Hybrid Z

By A.L.White

To my friend Steven Hernandez in Texas who has been a driving force in helping push me to finish this book.

Forced to leave the safety of Rivers Crossing, sisters Lori and Virginia, along with their vigilant guard dogs, Zeus and Perseus, find themselves on the road again, following Old Bob's map. Surviving the dangers of the zombie apocalypse has become second nature to them in this, the third installment of their adventure. Still, the ever changing virus, producing new and varied strains of horrors, continues to endanger them and their traveling companions. Perhaps the greatest danger travels with them, as Lori struggles to come to terms with her nature. The changes occurring within her threaten to tear the sisters apart, and destroy their search for a safe haven.

Chapter 1

The RV shifted to the right as the tires dug deep into the snow, finding the ice below. Walter behaved as though he didn't notice while the others braced.

"Sorry, was picking up a little too much speed for the conditions." Jermaine said looking into the rearview mirror at Lori and Walter. Sitting at the table they offered no reply.

After cleaning the blood off of Walter and sitting him down at the table, Lori sat opposite and looked at him, lost in thought. What little talk there was between Virginia and Jermaine, Lori did not notice. There were changes going on inside of her and she felt Walter was the only person who could supply the answers she needed.

"Why were you covered in blood?" Lori asked. Crinkling his nose, Walter shifted his gaze from Lori to the table without answering.

"Walter, I need to know why you looked like you took a bath in blood when we found you walking alongside the road. How did you get so far outside of Rivers Crossing?"

Walter shifted his eyes to the window and then back down to the table. "Walter," Lori repeated, "we need to know what is happening with you."

"What is happening to me?" Walter asked as his eyes rose to meet Lori's.

"Yes, what is happening? What are you going through?" Lori asked, prodding for more information.

"You want to know what is happening to you, Lori. You don't care what is happening to me." Walter replied.

Lori was speechless for a few minutes. *Do I care what is happening to the boy or am I worrying about myself?* She wondered.

"You don't know what is going on with me but you sure have a good idea. You know because you are starting to feel it too." Walter said.

"Feel what, Walter? Tell me what it is you are feeling."

Lowering his voice to where he felt only Lori could hear him, Walter replied, "You don't feel like we shouldn't be here? That we are in this camper with our food?"

"Yes, there is plenty of food for the trip to Clarksville and I hope there is more food there." Lori replied.

"That isn't the food I am talking about. That food tastes bland or has no taste at all for me. I want fresh food…food that has been taken down recently…It's becoming harder to turn away."

Lori found it hard to believe that those words were coming from such a small boy; a boy they took in and saved at the drive in theater only a few months ago. "You couldn't possibly mean that…."

2

"You feel it too! You know you feel it so don't lie." Walter yelled at Lori, then lowered his eyes to the table.

"Maybe sometimes…but we have to fight that until we figure out how to cure ourselves or…find a middle ground. We don't want to hurt our friends." Lori replied.

"We are new and they are old, don't you feel it?" Walter asked.

Lori shook her head, not wanting to believe anything like that. "Do you want to hurt our friends, Walter?"

Walter looked back out the window at the empty white fields passing by. "No, I do not want to hurt our friends…Sometimes it doesn't matter what I want, Lori."

Pushing back into cushion on the bench, Lori tried to become part of the fabric as her face went blank. She nervously tapped on the table as her eyelids became heavy and her breath involuntarily began to quicken. Her chest heaved and fell with shallow breaths. "We have talked enough for today. You look tired. Why don't you go in the back and take a nap, get some rest? I think we are getting closer to Clarksville and we can talk more about this when we get there."

Walter nodded in agreement, rose up from the table and gave Lori a hug, catching her off guard. She nearly jumped up defensively. Once he was in the back, looking down at the lads, Lori instructed Zeus, "Guard." She pointed toward the back. Zeus walked down to the narrow corridor leading passed the

3

bathroom and laid down staring towards the place where Walter was.

*****

Moving up the center of the street as silently as she could, she maintained a watchful eye on every doorway and cross street. The heat had come early this year and Megan found it to be unbearable to say the least. The stench from the rotting corpses all over town just added to her misery. At the corner of Main and second street, Megan came to a stop and focused on her feet for a few minutes then lifted her head slowly toward the old laundromat. More specifically her eyes lingered on the windows of the apartment above. Megan didn't think anyone would call the apartment nice by any stretch of the imagination. Affordable was about the only word that would describe the worn out old place. Part of her wanted to go in one more time and look around. Not that she would ever miss it. The apartment was a means to an end, having left home on her eighteenth birthday without worrying about money or food. She wound up working part time jobs with up to five roommates in a one-bedroom apartment. Any of them would be a welcome sight right now if they hadn't all turned soon after the outbreak. Looking down at the flaming red bite-mark on her arm, Megan could only wonder how long before she turned as well. The others seem to change within a day if memory served her correctly. Time had little meaning anymore; the days all ran together into one jumbled mess. They were all the same-looking for food or supplies during the day and hiding in an empty dumpster she found behind the Food Mart by night. It was the only one that had a medal lid which made it seem more secure.

Kevin Wallace, her sometimes roommate, had bitten her when she dozed off. He was the last to turn and Megan barely got free of his grasp. *Was he still in the apartment locked in the bathroom where she had left him? That was a week back, wasn't it?* The bite marks were still there, finally beginning to scab over. Her reflection in the old, small appliance shop window made it possible to see the bite on her cheek. It was deeper than the others but scabbing over just as well.

The sun was starting to set and Megan had spent far too much time standing in the same place. Heading down Second Street for the Food Mart and the safety of her dumpster, Megan could have sworn she sensed movement behind her. She stopped and surveyed but all was still aside from the swarms of flies feeding on the bodies in the street. Tomorrow morning she would do a better search of that area, just to be safe. Tonight she would button herself into the metal dumpster and endure the sweltering Georgia night.

Chapter 2

Six inches of snow covered a thin layer of ice, making forward progress hazardous and slow. The occasional drift crossing the road brought the trip to a near halt but slowly those too became visions in the rear view mirror. Charlie kept the Suburban in the middle of the road, trying to judge by trees or signs lining the highway. Jermaine fought the RV to stay within the tracks Charlie left, while Boo brought up the rear.

Overwhelmed by the endless white surroundings, Charlie was becoming mesmerized by the snow glistening in afternoon sun. He reached down and turned on the radio, only to be greeted by static. Nine hours on a trip that should have taken three on dry roads was taking a toll. Fighting to stay awake while struggling to stay focused on the white path ahead caused him to sometimes see things that weren't there; someone walking alongside the highway, a dog standing in the road or anything else his mind could dredge up from the past. Charlie knew that if they did not reach Clarksville soon they would need to find a place to stop for the night. He was tired, and there was no way he wanted to deal with the surprises that the dark would bring. They still had Lori who could take a turn driving. But that gave only one of them a rest, leaving the others to suffer on as best as they could.

Charlie could just make out what looked like buildings in the distance. Rubbing his eyes and blinking several times he tried to verify what he was seeing was real. *If Boo only knew the things he thought he had seen in the last few hours.* Sliding the vehicle a little to the left side of the highway, he focused more on the buildings.

"Ok, I will take the bait and bet my life that you are there." Charlie said to himself. Slowing to a complete stop, Charlie glanced back in the mirror noting the position of the RV and Boo's truck. He then took a quick survey of the emptiness around them. There were no trees for as far as he could see on either side of the road. Ahead lay the small town of Clarksville. Judging by their current rate of travel it was possibly another hour unless somehow they could pick up speed. The Suburban wasn't having any issues navigating through the four to six inches of snow, he thought it could easily handle picking up the pace. He had no doubt that Jermaine and Boo would do their best to keep up. The risk was that one of those two would lose traction on the ice and slide off into the steep ditch lining the highway.

A tap on the passenger window brought Charlie back to the moment. Lowering the window Charlie asked, "Want to take a break Boo?"

"I picked these up before we left the RV center yesterday, thought they might come in handy." Boo said handing binoculars into Charlie.

Smiling back at boo, Charley took them and climbed out of the truck, meeting him in front.

Focusing on Clarksville, Charlie quickly observed that it was smaller than Rivers Crossing. Maybe half the size, he thought, and that was being generous.

"Not much to it." Charlie said

Boo took the binoculars and focused in on what he thought was the main street. "What do you think is going on with them?" Boo asked.

"The cars in the middle of the street? Probably abandoned like all of the others we have seen." Charlie replied.

"Left them in a perfect line like that? I think they were traveling together just like we are. May want to move ahead with caution, Charlie. Something just doesn't seem right if you want my opinion, or even if you don't." Boo said.

"Would you feel better if we went down and took a look? Leave the others back here to keep an eye out?" Charlie asked.

Boo nodded his head and then said, "I would feel a whole lot better if we went down and took a look with Virginia and those dogs."

Charlie smiled. "If you would be so kind as to get Virginia and fill the others in, we can get this out of the way then. Getting darker by the minute and I would like to find a safe place for us to sleep."

Boo went back to the RV and returned a few minutes later with Virginia and the lads.

Zeus led the way with Perseus, as usual, walking right behind Virginia. She struggled to make her way through the snow on the single crutch Doc had given her. Charlie wasn't sure bringing Virginia was the best idea, but it was the only way to get the dogs to come along. They would have come with Lori, Charlie knew that. There was also the part of him that was beginning to have more than friendly feelings for Lori. He didn't want her to get hurt. Deep down, another part worried what would happen if zombies were present. Would Lori still be Lori or would something happen? He was in no rush to have an answer.

"Did Boo fill you in on what we're doing, Virginia?" Charlie asked.

"You would like the Lads to check things out so that you and Boo don't become dinner." Virginia replied.

"I think that about sums it up. I want you to stay inside of the Suburban just in case we need to get away quick." Charlie said.

Virginia glanced down at Zeus a little worried. No one else seemed to have noticed that Zeus was slowing down a lot in the last few weeks. His brain made promises that Virginia wasn't so sure his body could fulfill anymore. After Lori, Zeus and Perseus were like family. She couldn't bear to lose either one.

Boo helped Virginia into the back seat next to the dogs and they headed forward. The drive into Clarksville took less than twenty minutes without the RV. It was a small town, smaller than Rivers Crossing, which brought a smile to Charlie's face. It was kind of hard for him to believe that any place could be smaller. Two cars were stopped in the middle of the highway.

The tracks from the cars turned onto the highway from a street named "West Rd," just inside of Clarksville. Charlie followed until the snow went from white to a dull red color.

"Slow up a minute, Charlie. That's a lot of blood." Boo said.

"I don't see anyone around...or any bodies." Charlie said while bringing the truck to a halt.

"Virginia, it's time for the dogs to earn their pay." Boo said as he climbed out of the truck.

Opening her door and trying to make herself smaller than she was, Virginia instructed the lads. "Go check things out, boys."

Jumping over top of Virginia, Zeus and Perseus ran toward the red snow. Zeus, in his ever cautious way, was taking in all the sights and smells around him. Perseus charged ahead with little thought to anything other than beating Zeus there.

Zeus growled and nipped Perseus in the rear as he passed, causing him to slow up a little to keep pace with the older dog.

In the front of the cars Zeus found the people that had driven them and sat down waiting for Boo and Charlie to catch up. Perseus began checking out the fronts of the buildings on either side of the street. Virginia could tell that there were no signs of zombies just by how the dogs were acting.

Charlie's stomach was churning, working the acid up into his throat, as he passed through the bloody snow to the front of the cars. The bodies were laying in a messy line as if they had been lined up and fell to the ground. It took all that Charlie could muster to not vomit right there in front of Boo.

"Maybe they were surrounded and decided to end it all." Charlie said.

Boo continued looking around at the snow not paying much attention to the bodies.

"I think you're right about being surrounded, Charlie." Boo said moving off to the right towards an intersecting street. "I don't believe that it was zombies though. Most of the ones we have seen don't walk with a gait, they kind of shuffle along, dragging a leg or foot with them. More of a jerky type walk."

Charlie focused on the footprints in the snow and felt his stomach settle a little. "The smart ones, the two-point-zeros, walk fairly well."

"They don't drive vehicles, Charlie. These tracks were made by someone, or something, that can drive vehicles." Boo pointed at the street just ahead of them. "Came up from both directions and blocked the street right about there. Another set came out of that parking lot back there."

Charlie shook his head in disbelief at what he was hearing. "So on top of everything else we have a bunch of people preying on other people?"

Boo knelt down on one knee and pointed out the tracks around them. "That looks like they were made by the group in front of us. Right here are yours and mine, those belong to the dogs." Boo stood back up and looked at Charlie. "The rest of them look like they are all wearing the same type of boots."

"What do we do now?" Charlie asked.

"Hope like hell that they have moved on and we don't run into them." Boo replied.

Boo's thoughts were on everything around them as they drove back to join with the others. Every nook and cranny that something could be hiding in was looked over as he passed. Any places that they themselves could seek shelter in were noted and cataloged in his brain. Most would have thought that once out of town there was no place to hide for safety or for danger to be present. Boo could see spots in the vast, empty, white blanket of snow where a person or a group could have them within their sights; watching every move and waiting for the ideal moment to squeeze the trigger adding more lifeless bodies to the pile back in Clarksville.

*****

Finally convincing herself that she was imaging the movement down the street, Megan made her way behind the Food Mart to the large metal dumpster. She opened the metal lid and tossed her backpack in among the blankets that lined the bottom like a pile of dirty laundry waiting to be thrown in the washing machine.

It was far from the best accommodations in the world but it was the safest that she could find in the short amount of time that she spent searching the town. Megan had been leaving the lid open during the day so the heat didn't build up. That practice had to come to an abrupt stop yesterday when she climbed in and settled, trying to get as comfortable as one could in a dumpster, for the night. Lying there in the darkness she felt a tingle run across her left leg. Then it moved across the right leg and stayed there for a moment. It no longer felt

12

like a tingle but more like little feet and something long and thin. Digging into her pocket and finding the throw away lighter, she tried feverishly to light it. On the fourth try the flame lit up the pale grey walls and the glowing eyes of whatever was on her leg. Moving her other hand as slow as molasses towards the makeshift spear propped up in the corner, a ball of sweat built up on the tip of her nose threatening to fall at any moment, causing the momentary detente to come to an end. Locked in a stare with the rat she prayed that he would not move before he could be speared. Letting the lighter go out, Megan had been surprised by how aware she was of the creature. Even in the dark confines of the dumpster she could now see him and watch his every move. Something else came to mind too, an over powering urge to eat it. It was no longer a rat that had invaded her private safe place, it was warm and glowing in an aura that she could somehow taste as well as see. All of Megan's senses became acute, so aware that she could hear the tiny creature breathe, feel the patter of its heart on her shin, and feel her saliva building up at the thought of tasting fresh meat.

Tonight the thought of what she had done the night before was repulsive to her. Still something deep down had hoped that another creature would make the same mistake tonight. *If you truly believe that, then why did you shut the lid this morning? Now I have to lay in this hot metal box all night!* Megan thought to herself and laughed out loud until the sound of banging on the dumpster caused her to cringe.

"I know you're in there so come on out. No one is going to hurt you, girl." A deep male voice called from outside of the dumpster. Megan instinctively grabbed one of her spears and held it in front of her, pointing up at the lid.

"I have been watching you all day. If I wanted to harm you I would have done so while you were out in the open. I sure would not wait until you have that old piece of pipe with the sharp end on it nearby."

"Who are you and what do you want?" Megan asked while her mind raced for an idea to get out of the dumpster and find a safe place to run. The whole idea of the dumpster was to keep zombies away from her and it had worked pretty well. They couldn't open a lid and usually lost interest if she stayed still without making any sounds.

"Are you coming out or should I open the lid so we can talk like civilized people? I am not accustomed to standing in a dark parking lot talking to dumpsters." The voice stated without showing any sign of growing impatient with Megan.

Chapter 3

With darkness setting in there wasn't a lot of planning on what the next move would be. If followed, the map would take them through Clarksville then off to the east, to a farm just outside of town. Little was said about the bodies found on the main street as Boo felt it better discussed once they had settled in for the night. The sentiment was shared by the others after a brief explanation of the discovery. Dealing with creatures hell bent on eating them was one thing, wrapping their minds around survivors killing fellow survivors was another. It was a thought best left for later when they all had rested and were able to think with a clear mind.

Boo led the convoy in his old pickup, always staying at least fifty yards ahead of Charlie and Lori. *If they spring a trap on me the others will have time to take a defensive position or get out of here as best they can.* Boo thought to himself as he turned onto the road leading to the farm. Expecting to see headlights or armed men at any moment the entire way, he felt relieved when they turned into the long narrow snow covered road of the farm. Just short of the main house he pulled up and went back to the RV. Opening the door he jumped aside as the lads forced their way out of the door.

"The lads want to have a look around the place." Virginia said smiling at startled Boo.

"I was thinking the same thing walking back here." Boo said, smiling back.

Once Charlie came up from behind and they were all sitting in the RV, Lori unfolded the map and laid it across the table for them. Then, flipping it over, she pointed to the notes written all over the map.

"Bob left notes about most of the stops on the back of the map." Lori said. "I think he did this for Virginia and I because he would have known where everything was."

"It says right there that we need to go into the barn and look at the floor in stall three." Jermaine said.

"Maybe we can pull the RV and trucks into the barn if there is room like we did back at the first farm house?" Virginia asked.

"That would be a good idea if we could." Boo replied.

Lori started to fold the map back up. "I guess we should see if Zeus and Perseus have found anything and check out the barn."

The snow had stopped a day or so ago but they couldn't tell from what they saw. The wind was blowing across miles of open fields, picking up snow and creating a blizzard effect with each gust. The Lads quickly went to Virginia when she climbed out of the RV. They patiently stayed in a defensive position near her as she labored towards the barn as fast and as she could move while remaining stable.

"The door is locked!" Jermaine said.

Lori looked around the entrance. Seeing an old barrel by the corner, she went over and pushed against it to see if it was full. Judging it to be about a quarter full, Lori tipped the barrel on its side. Underneath was an old wooden tool box. Inside were a few old tools and a bronze box that said Bob on the lid. Opening it, she found a keyring with three keys on it. She tossed it over to Jermaine, catching him off guard as it bounced off his chest down into the snow. Jermaine smiled and wagged his finger at Lori before kneeling down to retrieve the key ring from the snow drift.

After the first two failed it was the third key that caused the locks to spring on the door. Jermaine pulled it open about twelve inches and looked back at Virginia questioningly.

"Zeus, Perseus, go!" Virginia said and the lads charged into the barn.

Jermaine opened the door wide enough for him to squeeze through followed by Charlie, Boo, and Lori.

The inside of the barn was cleaner than Lori was expecting. It looked more like a large auto repair shop than the last barn she had been in. The floor was concrete and clear of any debris, light blue in color with white lines painted along either side about a foot and a half from the ground. The lines led from the entrance way to what Lori was sure were stalls. Zeus and Perseus were sitting by one of the stalls. On closer inspection Lori laughed to herself and thought, *of course you have been here before, haven't you, boys?* Motioning to Charlie and pointing at the stall, Lori stepped back as Charlie slid the stall door open to reveal a wood floor with a handle sunk deep enough into the middle of the floor that it wouldn't cause anyone to trip over it when walking in. Charlie knelt down, pulling the door open and shining his flash light down the hole. Concrete steps descended down a level into a large open room. On the wall to Charlie's left he saw what looked like a control center. Lori walked passed Charlie and turned a key then pushed a green button. Light flooded into the room exposing what Lori thought had to be the main living area of the bunker. It appeared to be set up nearly the same as the first bunker only on a larger scale.

"You have to wonder just how many of these places Bob set up along the way." Virginia muttered.

"Not sure, there wasn't one in Rivers Crossing." Lori replied.

"Man! Will you look at this place here!" Jermaine said as he came into the room.

"Old Bob really put a lot of thought into these places. I guess he wasn't sure how long he would have to stay put." Lori replied still trying to take it all in. There was always the thought creeping into her brain about staying put. If there were enough supplies, they could take a break from the journey, allowing Virginia to heal a little more. She had to admit she could use the time on the mend herself.

"I don't know what you did down there, but the barn is lit up by low level red lights up here." Boo said leaning over so that they could all hear him.

Charlie went back up to the barn with Boo after explaining to the group that he would go help get the trucks into the barn and lock up for the night. The others had a peek at what was in the middle of the street. He on the other hand, had a bird's eye view and it still wasn't sitting well. Whatever or whoever did that could still be in the area and they were not too picky about what they killed.

"I am going to go ahead and pull the trucks in now." Charlie said to Boo when he reached the top of the stairs.

"Ok, I will give you a hand. Let's back the RV in first and then back the trucks in up front closer to the doors. That way if we have to make a fast exit we can use the trucks to plow a way for the RV to get passed." Boo replied.

Chapter 4

Rolling to his side, Charlie threw his arm over expecting to embrace Annie. The sudden memory of Annie's end brought him to an alert state. He looked around the room trying to recognize where he was. Seeing the others it all dawned on him, and he missed Annie more than he had allowed himself to in a long time. He had taken all of those feelings and locked them away in a room someplace in the far reaches of his mind. Feelings were popping up for Lori that, in truth, Charlie wasn't so sure he wanted to have. Those feelings brought Annie back to the front where she needed to be dealt with so that he could move on with whatever was left of his life.

Lori and Walter were missing from the room. Charlie jumped out of bed and went out to the main room where he could see the kitchen area. They were no where to be found and the door leading back to the barn was still locked from the inside, exactly how he had left it last night.

"What's all the excitement, Charlie?" Boo asked.

Charlie spun around on Boo and replied, "I think something has happened to Lori and Walter."

"Lori woke me up around midnight, said Walter wasn't feeling well sleeping by all of us. They were going to sleep in the RV and could I lock the door behind them." Boo replied.

Charlie calmed himself down knowing that the barn was not as secure as the bunker but fairly secure nonetheless.

"Go on and check on them if it will make you feel any better." Boo said motioning towards the stairs.

"I think I will Boo," Charlie replied as he headed up the stairs towards the steel hatch.

Once out in the barn the chill slapped him hard and he looked around for signs of Lori. The soft glow of a nightlight in the RV caught his attention. Rapping on the door he called out to Lori and Walter with no response. The door creaked as he opened it and he stuck his head in to find Walter smiling down at him from a bed that earlier had been the table.

"Good morning, Charlie," Lori said from the rear someplace.

Charlie climbed into the RV and sat next to Walter and said. "What made you two come out here in a cold barn to sleep?"

"Lori was having problems with the smell down there." Walter said.

Charlie didn't need any more explanation than that. More than once it had been obvious that the part of Lori that was…that was something else…tried to emerge when certain smells were too strong. Crammed into the lower area must have been too much to take.

Lori came out by Charlie holding a map. "Good morning, Charlie. Do you know if everyone else is up yet?"

Taking the map, Charlie could see the line running along the route that Bob had laid out for the girls to follow had now been joined by an alternate route separating at Clarksville. "I think they we all starting to move around after I made a little noise."

"Then we should go and talk to them." Lori passed by Charlie on her way to the bunker entrance. Walter took hold of Charlie's hand as he passed, pulling him along.

There were words that Charlie felt needed to be said between him and Lori. Words that were better said for now without the whole group being part of the discussion. If Lori and Walter couldn't stay in the same room as the others, then what did that hold for any future involving them? When Lori felt those feelings that caused her to abandon the warmth of the school back in Rivers Crossing and now here in the bunker, what was it exactly she felt? Charlie felt he needed to know.

"I see that Charlie found you two safe and sound?" Boo asked as Lori entered the main room.

Noticing that everyone had been awakened while he performed his search for Lori and Walter, Charlie said. "Sorry for waking everyone up this morning."

"That's fine man, not knowing just how much life I have left kinda makes me want to not waste it sleeping." Jermaine replied with a welcoming smile.

"I am glad you're all up." Lori said. "I was looking over Bob's map this morning and I think we can save some time if we bypass Terryville and head to Warm Springs, here." Laying the map on the table, she pointed to the red circle she had drawn around Warm Springs.

"I thought the plan was to follow the map all the way down." Charlie replied.

"I think the map is a guide to follow more than it is something etched in stone." Lori replied. "If we bypass Terryville we cut over three hundred miles off the trip."

"I am good with that plan, further south means warmer temperatures." Jermaine replied.

"Boo?" Charlie asked.

"I think between the supplies we have and what is here we would be good. There are enough emergency food packets here to feed us for a good while and more than enough extra firepower and ammo. So I think we could safely bypass Terryville." Boo replied.

Charlie looked over at Virginia and the lads questioningly.

"We go wherever Lori goes." Virginia replied.

Lori clapped her hands together and stated. "Then it is decided. I think we should start getting ready to leave while it's early."

"Maybe now is a good time to talk about what we found last night then. Before we head back out into the open." Boo said glancing over to Charlie.

The group had turned off before getting too close to the cars parked in the middle of the street. All the others had seen were the cars and what looked like bodies. Charlie had seen it up close and personal. It caused him more concern than it had the others. Lori, Virginia and Jermaine had become accustomed to bodies laying out in the open long before reaching Rivers Crossing. After a while the bodies all started to look the same, they became inured; sensitivity to that sort of thing, a moment's hesitation, it could cost them their lives.

"The people by the cars last night were executed." Boo stated looking at the faces of the others.

"Zombies?" Jermaine asked.

"Didn't look like it to me." Charlie replied "The dogs didn't act like they were either."

"Who do you think did it?" Lori asked.

"Looked like military boots to me, could have been some kind of militia though." Boo replied. "Thing is…" Boo started to say, then waited to finish when certain that everyone was listening. "Thing is that, if I go by the tire tracks in the snow of all the vehicles involved, it was definitely an ambush."

The room became silent while everyone felt the weight of the words Boo had just uttered.

"So on top of slow zombies and two-point-zeros hunting folks, now we have people hunting people?" Jermaine asked.

"For whatever reason it looks like someone out there is." Boo replied.

"Supplies?" Lori asked.

"It didn't look like anything was taken from the cars. Hard to say with any amount of certainty." Charlie stated.

"Last night there was talk about lessening the driving load by leaving my truck behind. I think instead of that, we should keep my truck and use it to scout out ahead of us." Boo stated.

"Like you did coming here?" Virginia asked.

"Yes, just like that Virginia. I will drive out about ten or fifteen miles ahead of the rest of you. If anything happens you take off in another direction if possible."

Lori shook her head no. "We will take turns scouting with another person and one of the dogs in the truck." Pausing to make sure that everyone understood what she was saying. "Bob had walkie talkies back there with the first aid kits. We can scout ahead as far as the range reaches on them."

Seeing that once Lori had made her mind up there would be no changing, Boo settled for the revised scouting plan. He would take the first scout, one of the dogs and whoever volunteered to ride shotgun with him. *It wouldn't be all that bad*, he thought to himself. At least he would have someone to talk to and another set of eyes watching the surrounding area

*****

Megan stood up with all her might, slamming the metal lid open. Like thunder, the sound of the metal lid slamming down against the side of the dumpster echoed through the deserted town. Standing there with sweat pouring off of her, she held her spear pointed at the man. The person behind the voice smiled back at her from a boyish, clean shaven face that looked odd with the large hulking body that it sat atop.

"There now, girl, isn't that better?" he asked. "Now then, what should I call you?"

Megan tried to take the surroundings in and find a way out if she needed it. If she could get out of the dumpster in one fluid motion, there was no doubt in her mind that she could out run him. She had always been faster than everyone else she knew.

"Would you prefer that I just make up a name for you?" he asked.

"Megan, Megan Lewiston." Megan replied.

Turning his back to her, the man sat back against another dumpster and asked. "How long has it been since you were bitten?"

"A few days, maybe a week." Megan replied as she lowered herself to the ground and sat. She was careful to keep enough distance between the two so she would have enough time to react if he sprang at her.

"Then I think it is safe to say that you will not be changing." He added.

"Do you think that I am immune?" Megan asked lowering her spear to the asphalt.

"Have you noticed anything different about yourself?" He asked as if he knew the answer.

Megan thought back to the rat from last night and how she seemed to be able to sense everything about it. Mostly she remembered how good the warm flesh had tasted.

"That's what I thought." He stated with a smile. "You are like me and the others I have been rounding up."

"Like you? What do you mean like you?" Megan asked picking her spear back up while her body tensed.

Motioning with his hands for her to calm down the man continued. "Do you believe in God, Megan? Do you believe that there is a higher power and a plan for everything that happens? A design by which creatures come into existence and then are replaced by better, smarter, and stronger creatures that can survive in the world?"

Megan thought for a few minutes and then shrugged her shoulders.

"Why do you think the pandemic happened? Why do you think that people like you and I have survived after being bitten? You yourself look like you were bitten several times yet here you are talking to me beside these dumpsters in the back of the local grocery store as if nothing has happened."

Megan shook her head and replied. "I don't follow what you're trying to say. Maybe we are just not affected by the virus or whatever it is."

"No child, we were affected by it. We are the new humans, the next step in evolution I think. There are more like us out there and I am trying to find all of them."

"Why would you do that?"

"Together we can build a new world, pick up the pieces and build a life again from the ruins."

"You want me to come with you?" Megan asked.

"No child, I want you to take that old ford pickup truck parked in the front of this store and head west on the highway until you come to a town called Hoopersville. There you will find others just like you and I. You pick them up, they will be expecting you, and head north towards a town called Clarksville. There are maps in the truck with the route marked out. Along the way you will find others who will join you. You bring them all to Clarksville with you, you hear me, girl?"

Megan nodded and started to ask when she should leave when the man continued. "The keys are in the truck so you best be getting on your way." He paused for a few minutes then added. "You will start to notice your body feeling different. Don't be alarmed…just enjoy the changes and remember them."

Megan got up and reached in the dumpster for her backpack. "There is nothing from your former life that you will need, including that damn pipe that you think will do you some good. There is a three-fifty-seven magnum in the glovebox with some ammo. That will keep you safe enough if need be."

Megan turned toward the side of the store trying to go over the entire conversation in her head. *The guy could be a whacko*, she thought. If he wanted to give her a truck and a gun, she would take it and follow his map. She'd find out soon enough if he was crazy or telling the truth. Either way, she was done with the town and couldn't wait to see it in the rearview mirror.

Chapter 5

Walking through the second floor hall, Doc noticed a surprising number of doors open. Normally at that hour people were asleep and the doors would be closed for privacy. There had been talk last night in the cafeteria about a safe haven out west someplace but he didn't pay a lot of attention. New folks brought in stories about mythical places where the government was helping survivors, where civilization was being rebuilt. There was no doubt in his mind that they had existed in the early days of the outbreak. However, there was plenty of doubt that any safe havens still existed that the Feds were running. Doc knew that there had to be more places like Rivers Crossing out there and more survivors. How long they would last was another story that he wished that he had an answer to. Pausing next to the room where Virginia and Lori had been staying, Doc found he missed them already. He missed Charlie and Boo as well, even if it had only been a day since they left. Yesterday he had regretted telling the girls that they had to leave and watching his friends make the choice to go with them. Today it was starting to look like the whole thing would have been a moot point if they had let it sit for twenty-four hours. From the looks of it, most of the people that had seen Lori as a threat had snuck off in the night, chasing the "safe haven" dream.

"Most of them are gone." Zoe said, startling Doc.

"I thought we might lose a few." Doc replied

"So did I, deep down. Prayed it wouldn't be, but deep down I think I knew they would leave. You can't stop folks from looking to get back to where they think they should be. Most days I still find it hard to believe that this is the new reality…that everything I knew and loved is gone and now part of a distant memory." Zoe said.

"Did you hear them leave last night?" Doc asked.

Zoe stared off into space then replied. "My nephew used to say that I could hear a pin drop down the street from my house. I guess I have always been cursed with hearing things that I would have been better off not hearing."

"I wish you would have woken me up so that I could have tried to talk to them." Doc said.

"Do you think it would have done any good?" Those folks thought they were safe here and then we lost almost half of them when the creatures broke through the barriers. If that wasn't enough for anyone to digest by itself, they then watched and helped gather up the dead and burn them. Doc, I don't think that anything you could have said would have meant much to them other than to say good luck and stay safe."

"I guess you're right, Zoe. We could have made a safe haven right here if they would have given it a chance." Doc said.

Zoe paused for a second and then asked. "Doc, do you know how to work the generator or the boiler?"

"I think Marvin and his boy do." Doc replied.

"Marvin was killed on the street out front and his boy was one of the ones in the school yard. Do we have anyone else?" Zoe asked.

Doc didn't want to think about it anymore. His process was to look at all the facts and make an informed diagnosis of the situation followed by a clear way to treat the issue. At the moment it was all pointing to the same conclusion, he was looking at a terminal patient with no treatment options. He could try to see if he could figure the generator out, take a whack at the boiler and hopefully keep the heat on. What Doc really wanted was a nice cup of coffee and a few minutes alone to collect his thoughts and decide what was best to do. The clicking of his shoes echoed through the empty stairwell until Doc found himself on the first floor next to the stairs leading down to the cafeteria. Pausing before heading down, the sound of his own breath echoed off the walls. Shaking his head in disbelief, Doc continued down the last flight of steps hoping that there would be some coffee left.

Tressa poured two cups of coffee, one for Doc sitting at the first table in the cafeteria staring down at the table silently, the other for herself. Placing the first cup down with a bang she gently set Doc's cup in front of him, sliding into his view. There they sat silently sipping at the coffee for the next twenty minutes until Todd came down the stairs. In his typical fashion, nothing that Todd did was quiet, and thanks to his size, it was never unnoticeable. He had found a parka that looked like it had been more at home in the seventies, a backpack with some kind of cartoon cat on it, and an old lunch box that Charlie had given him. Todd looked like he was planning to go on one of his adventures.

Tressa stood up and looked at her Uncle and wondered what he was up to. "Todd, are you ready to do your chores now?"

Todd walked right passed her, into the kitchen, slamming the swinging door into the wall on accident as he passed through.

"What's that all about?" Doc asked, finally looking up from the table.

"Not sure, but with Todd it usually means I am going to have my hands full." Tressa replied.

Tressa followed Todd into the kitchen where she found the open lunch box sitting on the counter. Inside there was three packets of instant hot chocolate, two juice boxes, and a package of saltine crackers that Todd had found while looking through the old Rivers Crossing shelter with Charlie and Virginia. Opening up the backpack Tressa found a comic book, sweat shirt, and a blanket. *This was not the typical Todd,* she thought.

"Todd honey, are you going to have an adventure without me?" Tressa asked. Todd froze with his hand in the box that he had hastily thrown on the floor. He was kneeling over it like a pirate, admiring the treasure inside. Tressa knew that sometimes when Todd got caught doing something that he thought she would not approve of he would freeze. It was as if Todd thought that if he stayed still she would not see him and just walk by. That and if he couldn't see Tressa then she wasn't there.

"Todd, I know you hear me, what are you up to?"

Slowly he turned and took the sight of Tressa in. Her face didn't look like he was in trouble so he thought he just might be ok. "I need to go, Tressa, those dogs are my friends and they will need me." Todd said

"We don't know where they are at Todd, there is no way for us to find them now."

Todd climbed up from his knees and grabbed a crayon out of the backpack. On the wall behind Tressa he drew a map for her. "They went down this street here, then they turned here." Todd said, looking at her face again to judge if the reaction was turning to anger. "Then," He stared at the ceiling before continuing, "They followed the road all the way until they come to a place called…."

"How do you think that you know this?" Tressa asked.

Todd changed from looking concerned to that big six-year-old smile he made when he thought he did something good and Tressa would be proud. "I was looking over the paper Charlie had in his truck."

"Todd, I told you that we can't just look through other people's stuff without asking first." Tressa replied.

"Don't be mad at Todd, Tressa, please don't. I wanted to make sure that the puppies were going to be ok is all, Tressa. I wasn't being sneaky or bad at all." Todd replied.

Tressa knew deep down that this was going to be a problem that would not just go away. Todd may be like a small boy but he was, in fact, a grown man, a very large, strong, grown man. Once he made his mind up it would be nearly impossible to persuade otherwise. This wouldn't be one of the things that she could offer an extra snack and another glass of hot chocolate to take Todd's thoughts off of it. It would return every time he thought about the dogs or Virginia. There was a sweet spot where Todd was at his best, that spot had involved Charlie, Virginia, and the dogs. Now it was gone. Deep down Tressa had dreaded when Todd would realize it. She worried that the day would be spent lying in bed crying at the loss of his new friends. That would have been bad, but this was going to be worse! There was no way to keep Todd under her protective gaze twenty-four-seven. One day she would not be able to find Todd and he would be out there with the creatures alone and scared. In the past just that thought kept Todd close by, barely letting her out of his sight for very long. Now Todd had a purpose in his mind to be away and that wasn't a good thing.

"Why don't we go talk with Doc?" she asked. Changing the subject, she forced the idea of Todd being out there alone out of her head for the moment.

"I have a lot of work to do, Tressa. I have to find some of those treats we found in that house for the puppies. I don't think they brought any with them and they love them." Todd replied.

"Doc lived here before the bad creatures came, maybe he would know where to find some of those treats?"

"Not just any treats, Tressa." Todd replied rolling his eyes as he headed out to find Doc. "They like the ones that look like little hotdogs in a bun."

Todd had a way of startling most people even when they knew him; flying at them with the excitement of a five-year old and the body the size of a professional linebacker. Not so for Doc. He had come to see Todd for what he was, an oversized child who tended to react like a child would. Doc grabbed his coffee cup just in case Todd slammed into the table, a lesson he had learned the hard way on more than one occasion in the past.

"Taking a trip, Todd?" Doc asked.

"Yes Sir, Mister!" Todd said with a large smile. "I am going to find the puppies and Virginia!"

"Well, you certainly looked dressed for it, Todd. It's going to be pretty cold and lonely out there."

Todd's smile faded momentarily. The thought process didn't cover the possibility of being completely alone until just that minute.

"I think we should find you some better shoes than those old gym shoes too." Doc added.

Todd turned his attention from being alone to his feet. "I think they will be ok. I have two pairs of socks on and some plastic bags! Tressa makes me where the plastic bags when I play outside sometimes."

"Why don't you finish your chores for Tressa and when you are done we will look and see if we can find you some proper shoes for your trip."

Todd's face lit up again. "Do you think we could?!" Todd said as he rushed forward and hugged Doc as hard as he could.

36

"Todd, why don't you go start your chores and let me talk to Doc so he knows what size shoes you need." Tressa said.

"I sure will, Tressa, I sure will! I am going to do my chores faster than anyone has ever done their chores. Do you think I can have some hot chocolate and the shoes?"

"I think we can work that out don't you doc?" Tressa asked.

"I was thinking that very thing myself. Maybe I will have some too, Todd." Doc replied.

"With the little marshmallows?"

"An extra helping." Doc replied.

Todd jumped up and spun around yelling "Yippee!" as he ran into the kitchen to start his chores.

"Thank you, Doc. You do know that he will try to go, right?" Tressa asked.

"Tressa, I have been thinking since this morning that maybe we should go. We might be able to catch up to Charlie in a day or so." Doc said

"You have heard the talk too?" Tressa asked.

"Yes, I have. Since Charlie and Boo left others are talking about a safe haven out west in Wyoming or Arizona." Doc answered.

" I had thought it was all just talk." Tressa said. "Zoe says the place is all but empty now."

"Pretty much from what I could see this morning making my rounds." Doc replied.

"Do you think it is true?"

I don't really know, Tressa. No one has a name or exact location of where this safe haven is supposed to be. It is all just rumors." Doc replied.

"You would rather try your luck with Charlie?" Tressa asked.

"I think I trust Charlie and Boo to get someplace safe, if that is what you are asking. If I am going to die chasing dreams I would rather it be with friends." Doc replied. "What I prefer to do is go out and find them and bring them back home."

Do you think they would come back?" Tressa asked.

Doc shrugged his shoulders. "I am not sure. I would like to talk to them and find out."

Tressa started toward the kitchen. "I will see what I can gather for the three of us to take with us. Can you see if you can find a good car or truck?"

Chapter 6

Doc found an old beat up blazer at Hanson's filling station a few blocks over. It looked as though the owner had gotten a new set of tires before everything happened. The poor guy never returned to pick it up. It wasn't pretty, but the motor sounded smooth and the tires looked great. As long as there was heat and a full tank of gas it would get them where they were going. If it couldn't make the trip back home, well, that was fine. They could hopefully ride back in the RV with Charlie and the others. Doc had to admit the prospect of leaving town was a little exciting, if only for a short while. Since the outbreak he had been in a two or three block radius of the schools tending to the sick and departed. Locally he wasn't known as one to head off on an adventure but he had his daring side. After all, he had closed his practice in Chicago and moved way out in the middle of nowhere to Rivers Crossing on a whim. How many other people could say that they were adventurous enough to walk away from everything they ever knew and start over? *Not many, that's how many*, Doc thought to himself.

Doc pulled up by the back door to the school and found Zoe, Tressa, and Todd waiting. Todd had on some kind of mixture of winter clothing, as if he were planning to walk to the North Pole. A sweat shirt, a hoody, a jacket, and not one, but two winter coats topped by a winter hat that pulled down over his ears and buckled under the chin. He was smiling from ear to ear as he noticed Doc pull in.

"Todd." Doc said as he exited the truck. "I think those plastic bags will do you more good inside of your boots, son."

Todd shook his head no and looked at Tressa.

"No, you explain the bags. It was your design." Tressa said.

"Miss Zoe found me some new boots. I don't want nuthin to happen to them." Todd said

"But Todd, I think the plastic bags are to keep your feet dry when you're out in the snow." Doc replied.

"That's why I have them mister, only I want to keep my new boots nice and dry too."

"Well, let's hope they stay nice and dry in the truck then." Doc replied.

Tressa moved Todd towards the door of the truck and helped him climb into the back seat. "You two stay safe out there and come back at the first signs of trouble. Looks like the flurries are turning to bigger flakes already." Zoe said

"There won't be no trouble, Miss Zoe, we're just going for a ride to get the pups, right Tressa? Just going for a ride in the truck to get the pups." Todd said from the back seat.

"Ok Todd, I hear you." Zoe Replied. "All the same, you two keep that in mind. I would rather have you here than dead someplace along the road."

"I promise you if anything seems to be going south on us I will turn right around and head for the safety of the school and my warm, dry bed." Doc said climbing into the truck. "Zoe, keep everything buttoned up here if you have to."

Zoe smiled and waved as Doc pulled away from the door.

"Doc, on the map it looks like it would be shorter to take this road along the river." Tressa held the map for Doc to see.

"That's the old river road, and you're right, it would be a lot shorter than taking the highway. Less likely to have any abandoned cars on it too, I would wager. The road was never in all that great of shape to begin with so most would avoid it." Doc replied.

Todd watched the white landscape pass them by slowly as the old truck made its way forward. Doc drove as fast as he could while complaining about the lack of visibility. Tressa, for the most part, ignored both as best as she could while trying to watch for things that she secretly worried that Doc would miss, like the edge of the road hidden beneath the snow.

"Tressa, can you keep an eye out for a small cabin off to the right?" Doc asked.

"Cabin?" Tressa asked. She was surprised at the thought of stopping so soon after their departure from Rivers Crossing.

"In the past three hours it has gone from bad to worse. I don't think it is going to get better as we go.

There is an old fishing cabin that we might be able to hold up in for the night and let this pass." Doc replied.

"A fishing cabin? A real fishing cabin? Please, can we stay there, Tressa? Please! I have always wanted to go to a real fishing cabin."

"I don't think we will be able to do any fishing, Todd." Tressa replied.

"Maybe not now, Tressa, but maybe someday we will." Todd said. "A real fishing cabin!" he added, excited at the prospect.

She pointed off into the wall of white and asked. "Is that it Doc?"

Doc nodded his head yes and maneuvered the truck off of the road, coming to a halt at what looked like it was a cabin at one time. The entire front was missing and part of the side too, but the roof and the other two walls remained standing.

"Once we make a fire I think it will be ok." Doc said, getting out of the truck. He walked around to the back of the truck and fished out the few bits of firewood he had packed for just such a need.

"Do you really think this place is safe, Doc? It doesn't look like we will have any cover from you know what." Tressa didn't want to say the creatures name and send Todd off into a rant or worse, a panic attack.

"I don't really think they are going to be out in this. Do you?" Doc replied.

"Why wouldn't they be out?" Tressa asked.

"Well, for starters, they don't seem to move very well on dry land or compacted snow. This out here is an easy six inches of fresh heavy snow. I just don't think they can move very well in it and we would be able to get away pretty easily. Doc replied.

"I am fast, Tressa. I can run really fast. I can show you. Do you want to see how fast I am?"

"No Todd, we can save your energy for when we need you to run fast." Tressa replied. She patted Todd on the back. "For now why don't you help Doc get a fire going and I will grab the sleeping bags we packed."

*****

Pulling out of the barn Boo became more aware of the black skies off toward Clarksville. It looked like they were going to get hit with one heck of a storm, he thought to himself. The flurries were beginning to be peppered with large, dime sized flakes. Virginia had talked her way into riding with him and Perseus for the first scout which didn't bother Boo all that much. He enjoyed being around Virginia because she did waste words on things that others would just to pass the time. She was kind of like him in that way, he thought, smiling to himself. It made him think of his boys and wonder how they had turned out or if they were even still alive.

The truck fish tailed breaking though a snow drift that had formed by the road heading back to town. Boo turned the wheel a little to the left, giving it just enough gas to right itself as he checked the rear view mirror to see how the RV had fared. Once satisfied that all were still with him, Boo began to speed up a little, putting some room between his truck and the rest of the convoy.

Turning onto the main street in Clarksville, Boo fixed the cars still sitting in the middle of the street in his sights. From there he could tell that it was no longer a neat little scene. Zombies had found the bodies or what was left of them. Creeping past it he didn't see any reason to stop Virginia from taking it all in. She had seen far worse in her young life than this. The only differences was it was originally the work of other humans.

"This is why we stay out in front of the rest?" Virginia asked.

Boo nodded his head yes to her, and tried to look for any movement on the sides of the street around them. The snow was coming down fairly heavy, covering the blood stained snow, leaving only the half-eaten carcasses exposed. Virginia pulled out the copy she had made of Bob's map and looked it over until they were passed.

"I think we turn to the right up here." Virginia said, pointing to a road just passed what had been a small convenient store.

"Uh-huh." Boo down shifted a gear and caused the pickup to slide into the turn. "How far up until we turn again?" He asked.

"It looks like we follow this road until we see the river and then head south along side it." Virginia replied, folding the map and petting Perseus who was looking out the back window for the others. Glancing in the side mirror she said, "I can't even see them anymore."

"The snow is so heavy the road is hardly visible in front too." Boo replied. He noticed he had been letting off the gas.

The flakes grew larger while the wind picked up, creating a near total whiteout. Boo kept driving forward hoping that the others were keeping up. Knowing that the idea of scouting ahead wasn't doing anyone any good without visibility he thought about pausing until Charlie caught up. Sliding to a stop when he could make out the river twenty yards ahead of him, Boo wiped a little sweat off of his brow. "That was a close one." To the South he knew there was nothing ahead of them but open road with a few pull off spots where people used to go fishing and have picnics. To the North there was an old pavilion that could be used for shelter if needed; three sides had bushes grown up leaving just one way in or out facing the road.

Boo put the truck into reverse and let the clutch out, spinning the tires at first until they found traction. With the truck pointed in the right direction he eased it forward, trying to find both edges of the road.

"It's pretty out here." Virginia said.

"Looks like a picture postcard for some place." Boo replied, smiling at her and Perseus.

"Do you think the snow will let up any?"

Boo looked towards the sky as best he could in the blizzard conditions. "I am not so sure the snow is our problem right now. Looks like the wind is picking up all the snow that we had and mixing it in with the new."

Virginia nodded in agreement. A crashing sound emanating from the driver's side startled them before the impact had its full effect. Boo's was knocked over on top of Perseus as the truck slid off the road into the ditch.

"Out of the truck now, head into the woods with Perseus until I call out for you!" Boo ordered Virginia as he leaned back up into his seat. He shifted, looking out into the snow for what hit them. Back up on the road he could make out what looked like an old tow truck, the bumper and grill showing signs of the collision.

"Boo, I…"

"Girl, get into the woods and take cover with the dog. Keep him quiet if you can until I come get you. Please." Boo replied. "Stay as low as you can and move as fast as you can."

As soon as he saw that Virginia was dashing toward the woods as fast as her crutch and determination could carry her, Boo pulled out his forty-five and started trying to force his door open. It groaned at each pop with his shoulder until it gave way, creaking as it opened. Climbing, out he searched for signs of a driver. The tow truck was empty and any tracks the driver left were covered before Boo had reached the driver side door. Moving back to his own truck he surveyed the damage. It looked a lot worse than he had thought. The front tire had been forced off the rim by the force of the collision and the rest of the truck looked like it was bent into a banana shape. There was no way the truck could move. He and Virginia would have to wait for the rest of the group to catch up.

Boo's mind was already thinking, he needed to make sure the rest of the group didn't pull up into a trap when they arrived. Walking around to Virginia's side, his lips moved to call out to her when he felt a sting seconds before hearing the shot that tore through his right shoulder nearly ripping his arm off. Falling face first into the snow, Boo used his right arm to push up on the ever growing red, slushy snow that he was laying in. Once he was nearly to his feet, another shot struck him in the lower back, kicking him forward to the ground again. Over the throbbing of his pain Boo heard the thwock of the crossbow as it let a bolt fly. He looked up in terror at the idea of Virginia taking on the unknown person out there. A thud hit the ground someplace behind him and he felt Perseus licking his face.

"Here Boo, let's get you up." Virginia said, pulling his good arm up off of the ground. Helping Boo over to the truck, Virginia found whatever she could use to stop the bleeding.

"Take that old blanket and cut it into strips." Boo said. Then we can try to tie it off around my shoulder and my back as best we can."

Virginia did as she was told, but there was too much blood and it wasn't showing signs of slowing.

"Ok girl, that looks like you have it as good as it's going to get for now." Boo said. "I need you to help me into the woods with as many of the things in the cab you can give me to keep warm and protect myself."

"I am putting you back into the cab with the motor running." Virginia said.

Boo grabbed a hold of her and gently pulled her so that she could look him in the eyes. "We don't know how many of them are out here and we don't want them surprising the others like they did us. If you leave me in the cab, then they know one of us is here and the other is on foot. Hide me in the woods where I can see them come up and I might be able to pick them off or slow them down."

"Where will I be?" Virginia asked. She sounded afraid. Boo had never heard fear in her voice before.

"You're going to take this dog here, and go down by the river and make your way back up north. Listen for the others as best you can. When you hear them, and only when you hear them, you come back up to the road and warn them away from here."

"I don't like it but I will do it." Virginia replied. She helped Boo down through the snow filled ditch and into the woods. She found a large tree, partially hidden from the road, where Boo would be able to see traffic up by the truck and keep himself somewhat hidden. The truck didn't have a lot of supplies in it but she found some old blankets and rags to help keep him warm. All of the ammunition for his forty-five and rifle were left in easy reach by his good arm and the weapons she tucked carefully onto his lap. After making sure they were loaded and the safeties off, Virginia said. "If you're sure about this we're going to head up river now."

She had seen enough death to recognize it knocking at his door but she wasn't about to disrespect the man she admired so much by disobeying his last orders. She called Perseus to her side, gave Boo a smile and a nod, and headed off to warn the others.

Chapter 7

Following the map the man had given her outside of her dumpster, Megan kept moving north through small towns and villages. The temperature had dropped from unbearable to comfortable and finally it was swinging to chilly. Most places had no signs of life, just a few groups of dead milling about. They would turn toward her, making a labored move to investigate, then just stand there watching her from behind black eyes. They were the same people who would have looked down their noses at her a year ago, judging her by the clothes she wore and her tats. *Now who were they looking down on?* She had survived and they didn't. It was if God looked down from the heavens and punished the ones who thought that they could judge others.

Just outside of another little town with another name that pretended to be a far off exotic place, Megan found a small strip mall filled with high end shops. Pulling into the parking lot, she looked for signs of trouble. She saw nothing that would concern her so she grabbed the pistol out of the glovebox and decided to going shopping. First she would find some new clothes to wear and then drive through the neighborhoods looking for a place to get a shower. Megan couldn't remember the last time she had felt the caress of warm water across her body. There had to be an odor clinging to her body that by now she was accustomed to. She thought it would be nice to start the next leg of the trip in some clean clothes on a clean body.

Looking through the windows of the first shop, she stared at the walls lined with dresses and blouses that would probably have looked wonderful on her grandmother. Megan moved to the next shop which by the looks of it was a resale shop. She looked down at the worn out jean shorts she was wearing. The pockets were hanging out from under where she had originally cut them. *I have lived my entire life wearing hand me downs, why stop now?* Looking around, she saw a tall, thin metal cigarette butt holder. Tucking the gun into the back of her shorts, Megan lifted the container up over her head and slammed it into the glass door. A thud, followed by a clang, echoed as the container bounced harmlessly off the glass, coming to rest at her feet, spilling its treasure of butts and ash all over the sidewalk. Quickly looking up one side of the strip mall and then down the other, Megan half-heartedly expected someone to come out and check on what the noise was. Seeing no one, she reached out for the door and shook it violently. She hopped back with a start as it pulled open with ease. *Of Course, you're not locked so I just looked like a complete fool for nothing at all.*

Most of the clothes by the entrance way were for summer. She had never been up north so Megan wasn't exactly sure of how to dress. One thing she did understand was that short shorts and a crop top weren't going to cut it. *I would make it look hot though,* she thought with a smile.

She moved back through the middle of the store, taking in all the different styles of clothes. She came to a round rack with jeans that were in her size. Grabbing a few pairs, she walked up to the counter in the back and laid them next to a corpse draped collapsed at the check out.

"Can you watch these for me please? I have some more shopping to do." Megan said to the corpse and then laughed aloud. "Thank you, sugar."

She found a few shirts that looked like sweat shirts but seemed to be a lot thinner. She took them back to the counter and laid them down. The corpse was about seventeen or eighteen when it had been living, Megan guessed. Beautiful flowing red hair was matted in the middle by a clump of reddish-black goo. Long and slender, it was dressed in clothes that were easily bought from someplace else, a place a little higher end than the resale shop. Megan loved the top it had on and started to figure out how she would get it off the body. Feeling the stiffness with a gentle poke told her that it wouldn't be an easy thing to do. In the mirror next to the cashier counter Megan noticed the patch of red in the middle of her tank top, starting just below her chin, running down to about the middle of her stomach. Remnants of her friend mister rat, she thought to herself and started to pull the shirt over her head slowly, watching herself in the mirror. *The stiff on the counter may have had better clothes but she could never stand and go toe to toe against my body,* Megan thought.

"Should I come back or is it ok if I just stand over here and watch quietly." A voice behind her startled Megan and she jumped up, reaching for the gun tucked into the back of her shorts with one hand and covering her chest with the other. Slamming down hard on the floor, the gun sent an echoing thud through the shop.

"Easy there Megan, I was told to find you and I mean you no harm." The owner of the voice raised his hands up to show he was not armed.

Megan bent forward grasping the gun and raising it towards the boy in front of her. "Who told you to find me?" Megan asked.

"Some dude that found me in my families barn a few nights ago."

"What was his name?" Megan asked.

"He never said and come to think of it, I never asked."

"What did he look like?" Megan asked growing impatient.

"Big guy with a baby face, dressed from head to toe in black."

"What is your name? Why should I believe you?" Megan prodded.

Lowering his hands down to his side, the stranger said. "The Man in Black said that I should find you here. Your name should be Megan. My name is Winston Salem the Third, but you can call me Bubby. Everyone has called me that since the day I was born."

"Isn't Winston Salem a town? Megan asked.

"It sure is, no fooling you is there? It seems that my grandfather was conceived there and so was my father. Hence we were all named that." Bubby replied.

"So you were too?" Megan asked trying to hold a smile in.

"Nah, my old man was way too cheap to take my mom anyplace, even before they were married. I was born up the road a little way in the same bedroom I have lived my whole life. I guess dad just wanted to keep the tradition going as best he could in his own way."

Megan lowered the gun and stood there looking at Bubby with her hands at her side. "Help me get this top off of the stiff."

"That will be way too thin if you get my meaning." Bubby replied looking down at his shoes as his face turned crimson.

Megan decided that he was probably right and the whole idea of going in the store had been to get something that didn't smell like death. Absentmindedly she grabbed a T-shirt from a rack next to her and put it on. "I want to get a shower before we leave this town"

"I can do better that that! How would you like a warm shower and a swim in an Olympic sized pool?" Bubby asked.

"You're on, afterward we will start following the Man in Black's map again."

****

Doc had Todd help dig a fire pit and area to sit in the middle of what had been the old fishing cabin. The remaining walls of the cabin were blocking the brunt of the winds from blowing the snow like tiny nails into their exposed flesh. Todd used an old cooler lid he found to push all the snow he could move while Doc lit a fire. Tressa carried the sleeping bags they had salvaged from the old hardware store on Main Street and a few cans of baked beans over to the fire pit.

"The fire is going nice, it is starting to get nice and toasty." Tressa said.

"Are we going to have toast for dinner, Tressa?" Todd asked confused.

"No Todd, it is nice and warm here." Tressa replied laughing.

Doc unrolled the three sleeping bags around the fire and sat down, leaning against the thick evergreens that grew where a cabin wall once stood. "Good thing these are water proof." He said, reaching into his pocket and pulling out a pack of smokes. He offered one to Tressa.

"No thanks, I am good, Doc." Tressa replied, fishing in her coat pocket for the can opener.

"Good for you, these things will kill you." Doc said as he took a piece of kindling and held the end into the flames. Once it caught fire he pulled it out, using the burning tip to light the cigarette. He then tossed the kindling it into the fire.

"Are you sure it will be safe here, Doc?" Tressa asked looking around at the openings in their temporary shelter.

"I don't know about you but I had a hard time moving through that snow from the truck to the cabin.

How did you feel when you were making your way in here?"

"I will give you that, it isn't very easy moving through the snow but—"

Doc cut her off, "Exactly! We move about pretty well normally, right? The creatures shuffle along, having a hard time. I don't think they will move very well at all in this weather, or in all of the built up snow."

"So you're saying that we are safe for tonight?" Tressa asked smiling.

"No, I am guaranteeing that you are safe for tonight." Doc replied

"Whaaaaaat are you doing, Tressa?!" Todd asked excitedly as Tressa carefully placed the opened can of beans into the edge of the fire.

"I am cooking the beans for dinner, Todd."

"Haven't you ever roughed it, my boy?" Doc asked.

Todd shook his head back and forth in disbelief. "We have never ever cooked like that before, have we, Tressa?"

"Well, this is what you call roughing it, Todd. We don't need any pans because we can just cook in the cans." Doc explained.

"Are we going to have spoons?" Todd asked. "I don't think I can eat without a spoon or fork, Mister."

"I brought utensils, Todd." Tressa used a pair of tongs to pull the cans of beans out of the fire, placing one in front of everyone. Todd laid flat on his stomach, propping his upper body up with an elbow so that he could eat from the can without touching it.

"Will we find the puppies tomorrow, Mister?" Todd asked with a mouthful.

"Todd, no one wants to see your food. Chew your food, then talk." Tressa scolded him.

Todd forced himself to swallow the mouthful of hot beans then asked again. "Do you think we will, Mister?"

Doc leaned back into the evergreens and pulled the pack of smokes out again. "Well, I don't think they could move tonight either so they are probably hunkered down just like we are. So I can't promise that we will find them tomorrow, Todd. I can say that I don't think we have fallen any further behind."

"Mister, does that mean we will find them tomorrow or not?" Todd asked again.

"Todd, mind your manners now. Doc doesn't know if we will find them tomorrow any more than you or I know it." Tressa said.

"Aw jeez Tressa, you don't have to get mad. I was just askin' is all."

Doc looked up at the weather worn roof of the cabin wondering how much snow it could hold in its dilapidated shape. "Todd, I am in just as big of a hurry to find the group as you are, son."

"Really Mister, you're in a hurry to find the puppies too?"

"I think he wants to find the whole group, Todd." Tressa replied laughing, causing Todd to laugh too.

Tressa wished that life could always be like that. Todd was so calm since they departed Rivers Crossing on their quest for the dogs. Doc seemed to always know what to say and how to say it to Todd. He always drew a calmer response than others did.

"Mister, are you ok? You don't look so good do you?" Todd asked.

Todd's voice called Tressa back from being lost in her own thoughts. Doc's eyes were bulging to the point that Tressa was worried that they just might pop out of their sockets. "Doc, are you ok?" She reached around the fire toward him. "Are you choking on something, Doc? Can you hear me?"

Doc opened his mouth to speak but words didn't form. Instead he let out a gargling sound, his neck beginning to bulge like his eyes. Tressa looked at Todd. "Go to the truck now and wait for me inside!"

"What is wrong with him?" Todd asked looking scared. "What is wrong with you, Mister?"

The bulge in Doc's neck ruptured, exploding outward with the spray of crimson blood, painting everything in the cabin in a bath of red. Doc's neck rendered aside, Tressa could see white fangs clicking together amidst viscera. Doc's body was then ripped from the cabin through the evergreens.

58

Reaching over to Todd she grabbed him by his ear, pulling him to his feet. "To the truck now!" Todd's arms and legs flailed as he ran through the snow, kicking up chunks of snow in every direction while he screamed at the top of his lungs. There was a brief pause in his scramming as he slammed into the side of the truck door. Tressa opened the door and pushed him inside. She kept her eyes on the creatures mauling Doc's body as she moved to the front door and tried to pull it open. The old hinges made a loud cracking then groaning sound as it opened. It attracted the attention of one of the creatures. It turned toward the new food source and fell onto all fours, charging toward Tressa. Calmly pulling the revolver out of her coat, Tressa squeezed off the shot just as the creature started to leap at her. It fell, what was left of it, just inches away from her snow entrenched feet, dead. She climbed into the truck and as more of the creatures noticed her, slammed the door shut.

"Lordy Tressa, what are they?" Todd asked with his nose pushed against the window. "They look like puppies, Tressa. But I don't think that they are."

Tressa didn't know what they were and she didn't want to find out what they were. As long as they were outside of the truck and she could get away, she was satisfied.

The door on Todd's side smashed as Todd began screaming with tears flowing down his face. "They're getting in, Tressa! They're getting in. Help me!"

Tressa started to raise the revolver but then instinctively reached for the keys in the ignition. After what felt like hours of fumbling around the steering column they found the ignition but there were no keys. *Doc put them in his pocket,* she thought looking out at the creatures milling around the truck.

"Tressa, lets go, please, can you drive us away from here, please?" Todd continued to plead between sobs.

Looking around at the creatures Tressa thought there were possibly six, maybe seven, of them. She tried to judge the distance to Doc's body or what was left of it. Tressa lifted the revolver and opened the cylinder. She had just five shots left for six or seven creatures. Who knew if there were more out there beyond the trees. *Could I shoot five and get past the last two?* She wondered. *If I make it to Doc, how long to find the keys in that pile of flesh and bones?*

Tressa moved over closer to the window on the passenger side and looked the creatures over. They weren't like the slow zombies, but they were not like the two-point-zeros that the girls had talked about. They were taller than a Great Dane but nearly as long as a tiger or lion. Their heads were elongated as if they were pulled that way by someone, causing they eyes, ears, and snout to be enormous. The fangs were large like something out of a book of drawings on prehistoric mammals.

"Tressa, lets go please, can you drive us away from here, please?" Todd begged again.

"Todd, I want you to lay down in the seat and take a nap for me." Tressa said.

"Take a nap, Tressa? I can't take a nap now!"

"Todd honey, I think if we stay very, very still and don't look at them they will just go away. Then we can get the keys from Doc and go." Tressa explained.

Todd wiped his eyes and laid down in the seat. "If it will make the bad things go away I will try, Tressa."

Tressa laid down across the front seat holding the revolver in both hands as she tried to sink into the fabric.

Chapter 8

Zeus was the first into the snow when the RV stopped by Boo's truck. Searching the area around the truck, in the truck, and then sniffing the body in street Zeus hadn't found Boo, Virginia, or Perseus. Zeus turned his search to the area behind the tow truck before charging into the space on the other side of Boo's truck. He covered the area, going back and forth, until he picked up a slight scent. Running through the snow up to Boo, Zeus sniffed him and knew that he was dead. He turned his attention back to the two trucks on the road. He didn't find Perseus or Virginia. He doubled back, following Lori as she headed toward Boo. He was sniffing the air intently for any scent trace of Virginia.

"What the hell?!" Jermaine asked as he checked Boo.

"Any signs of my sister or Perseus?" Lori asked.

Charlie shook his head no as he looked up from Boo to Lori's eyes. "There is another guy up there with an arrow through his eye."

"We know they're alive then." Walter added.

"Alive and on the run…or did someone or something get them?" Lori asked as Zeus caught a slight scent of Virginia toward the river. He Darted off at full speed, following the trail the best he could through the snow.

"Where is he going?" Charlie asked.

"I think he picked up their scent." Jermaine replied. "Should we follow?"

"In this mess? I think we should take the truck and drive back up the road slower. Maybe we will see them or they will see us." Charlie replied.

"Maybe take the RV? There is more room once you do find them." Lori said.

Jermaine looked back up at the RV and truck and shook his head. "May be a little harder to get her turned around but it could be doable."

"I think the two of you could manage it." Lori replied.

"Let's get going then." Jermaine said as he glanced over to Charlie who nodded in agreement.

"What about us?" Walter asked.

"You and I are going to have a little talk about our…new found abilities." Lori replied as her eyes watched Jermaine and Charlie make their way back to the RV.

"What about him?" Walter asked pointing at Boo.

"Walter, what do you feel about the others?" Lori asked.

"I like all of you. You have been very good to me since I met you."

"Where did we meet you at Walter?" Lori asked.

Walter looked to the sky for the answer and then to the river. "I don't remember, Lori. Alongside the road I think." Walter replied.

"Let's come back to that one, OK? For right now run up and see if there is a blanket or something in the truck behind the seat." Lori stated.

"Are you cold?" Walter asked amused.

"No, I want to cover Boo up." Lori said looking at Walter cross.

"Cover him up!?"

"Yes, that is what you do to show respect." Lori replied.

"I liked this one more than the others but he is dead now. Dead and still very fresh!"

"What do you mean still very fresh?" Lori asked.

Walter shuffled his feet around a little bit and then replied. "You have to smell it too right? Those people aren't like us."

"Those people are my friends and family, Our friends and family." Lori replied.

"Nothing is the same now, Lori. People have changed. You and I have changed to be part of the new."

"New?"

"Before everyone was like everyone else. Now there is new and we are new." Walter stated growing annoyed with Lori.

"You mean..."

"Yes, I mean that. To us they are food and that is all they can ever be." Walter replied.

"I can't except that, Wally." She said it knowing that being called by that name would bother Walter. Surprisingly, it didn't bother Walter in the slightest bit. The part of his brain that would have been set off by the nick name wasn't functioning anymore. He no longer remembered anything long term. Lori doubted that Walter could remember very much anymore. She had noticed that on occasion Walter wasn't even sure where he had met her or if she was his mother or not. Other times he seemed to recall clearly. Being in constant danger seemed to stay with him. Finding food, and remembering where he had seen food, stayed with him always. Sometimes he would try to remember what the face of his mother had looked like before all of this had started. There were blurred visions of a kind looking female but he couldn't be certain that was her. It could have been Lori or Virginia as far as Walter knew.

"You see everyone as food?" Lori asked.

"You do too, Lori. I see how your eyes gloss over and go grey like mine do." Walter replied growing impatient with her. "Look at your skin and then look at their skin. They are soft and kind of tasty while ours is growing grey and kind of hard."

Lori couldn't deny anything that Walter was saying. Her skin was starting to grow hard to the touch and the shade did seem to change every day to a grayer color. Did that make it absolute that she would one day turn on her friends, turn on Virginia and try to eat them? There had to be a middle ground that she could cling to that would keep everyone safe. Still, she too could smell Boo's flesh turning to a state that she suddenly found to be unappealing. The urge to take a small bite was growing stronger in Lori the longer that they stood by. She knew the same urge was growing in Walter too, that they should retreat back up to the truck before things went too far to explain to the others.

Walter stepped closer to Boo and knelt down beside him. "Stop! Let's go back up by the truck for now." Lori ordered. Walter looked over at Lori and a low growl escaped him. She narrowed her face and stared into his eyes until Walter relented and headed back toward the truck, sulking.

*****

Megan moved through the river of rotting flesh, unsteady and wobbling, toward the truck. She was wincing a little with every step feeling as though a knife was buried inside of her skull. Skin hung from the faces, eyes sunken, glossy, grey and lifeless. The smell no longer caused the burning sensation inside her nose. Either she was growing used to it or she now smelled like them. It didn't really matter. The man in black had told her to take the truck and meet him up the road with the others. That had been three weeks ago. She wanted to go alone, having begged for the Man in Black to let her come to him by herself, and lost. Megan looked over the travel companions before her. There were no signs of the change becoming permanent that she could see. Having been the Man in Black's favorite since nearly the beginning, she was feeling it slip away. It wasn't helping her headache. The one called Liza was taking the honor away with perfect blue eyes and cascading blonde hair. The world was moving on from the time of humans, becoming their time. Here again she felt like an outsider.

"Get in the truck." Megan said as she opened the driver's door.

Liza went around to the passenger side door with a guy Megan thought was called Peter. "You ride in the back with the others."

"Why do I have to ride in the back? It's cold out here, I will freeze back there." Liza replied.

Megan looked Liza in the eyes and tried to calm herself. Rage was boiling up from deep within to the point that Megan knew there would be no return. It wasn't so much that she hated Liza. She wasn't even jealous of her when she really thought about it. There was something with becoming. This new being that was transforming her. The shy loser that hung out on the outside of her circle of acquaintances cursed by a shyness that knew no boundaries was changing. "Maybe you can bring that up to Man in Black if you make it there." Megan replied

Liza knew what that meant and she wasn't ready to push things with Megan. In a child's attempt to get the upper hand before retreating to the cold truck bed she said, "That's fine by me, you stink something horrible anyway. I would have to hang my head out the window the whole way just to breathe."

Mega turned the key and forced the old Dodge into gear and started through the herd. She gave them a chance to move out of her way, if they didn't, the truck plowed over or through them.

"It's amazing that we can just walk among them." Peter said

Megan didn't want to talk to him or the others. *Why do they always feel the need to talk and question all of this?* She wondered to herself.

"A few months ago if I would have seen a herd this size, I would have thought I was screwed royal." Peter added. "Do you control them?"

Megan stopped worrying about hitting zombies and looked toward Peter. "How do you control something that is dead?"

"You can't, but then how do we move among them without being attacked?" Peter asked.

"I don't know, maybe they think we are them, maybe they like us? I really don't know. We just do is all I can say about it." Megan replied

"Does the Man in Black control them?"

Megan thought for a few minutes before answering Peter. It was a good question that she had wondered about herself more than once. "I don't think so." She replied.

"Peter, do I stink?" Megan asked.

Peter started to laugh and then replied. "Is this a trick question? If I answer wrong will I get banished to the back of the truck?"

Megan smiled. "No, I was just curious is all. Never mind."

"Oh, you're asking because Ms. Snooty said that you stink. I don't think you smell any more than the rest of us do. Liza doesn't really seem to be getting it." Peter replied.

"The sky is really black up ahead of us." Megan said wanting to change the subject.

"Looks like one heck of a storm is coming. I bet we get a foot of snow or more." Peter replied.

"I hope it holds off until we get to Clarksville and meet up with the Man in Black."

Chapter 9

Tressa didn't know if twenty minutes had passed or if it had been two hours. The clock didn't work in the beat up, old truck and she didn't own a watch. She listened as hard as she could for sounds of movement outside but could only hear the deep breathing of Todd in the back seat. *At least he was staying still like she had asked him to,* she thought.

"Tressa." Todd said in a hushed tone.

She thought if she stayed quiet and acted like she couldn't hear him he would go back to being silent. But she knew that would never work with Todd and it didn't.

"Tressa, are you still up there?" Todd asked a little louder. "Tressa, I am really cold and I think I need to go."

"Todd, we have to be really quiet, remember?"

"I know we have to be really quiet and not make any noise. I remember you said that, Tressa, yes you did. But I have to go and I am so cold my teeth are chattering." Todd replied. The window above Todd's head cracked loudly when the creature smacked into it. Tressa swore she could hear each path the cracks took as they traveling through the glass.

"Tressa! They are getting in. They are getting in!" Todd screamed, attracting the rest of the creatures back to the truck. Claws scratched against every window except the windshield, leaving long scores in the glass. As the wails began announcing that Todd was about to let loose of a very loud and prolonged crying fit, the front of the truck felt like it dropped. With a loud bang of metal, something gave way beneath a greater force. Tressa slowly sat up cradling the pistol tight against her chest. There, separated from her only by the windshield, was a creature. Its eyes were locked onto her like a cat's eyes locked onto a mouse just before pouncing. Tressa felt like the creature could see inside of her and was sucking out her soul. The skin around its muzzle barely fit over the teeth protruding from its gaping maw. Saliva dripped from the largest set of fangs that Tressa had ever seen. She didn't know if the windshield would stop the beast if it charged or if she could take it down with a bullet. *Would the others then charge as well?* She wondered.

"Todd honey, you really need to help me and try to be quiet." Tressa begged.

"Tressa, they are going to eat us! Can't you make them go away please." Todd replied, crying even louder than before.

Raising the gun slowly up with both hands until it was aimed at the creature's head, Tressa tried to swallow but couldn't, as she slowly pulled the hammer back. The creature moved a little closer and took one massive claw, tapping it on the window as it looked into her eyes. Without warning it slid the claw down to the bottom of the windshield and pulled the wiper off with a slight flick.

Pain was beginning to sting in Tressa's forearms from the weight of the pistol and her fingers were growing numb from squeezing the grip tighter than she had ever gripped anything before. Beads of sweat from just below her hairline slid their way down into Tressa's eyes, causing her vision to blur. Tap, tap, tap. The sound from the left side of the truck caused her to momentarily shift to her eyes only to find another creature standing on its hind legs with front paws up against the window tapping at her with equally massive claws. Coal black, lifeless eyes seemed to beckon to Tressa to give it up, open the door and accept her fate. Drawing its mouth open, the creature roared with such intensity that it felt like the truck shook in fear. Returning to look at the creature perched on the hood, she found it laying, its eyes glued to her. Tressa thought they may catch a break even with Todd crying. If they could just keep still, if Todd would just stay still, the creatures were getting used to his cries and starting to settle down, seemingly content to wait for their dinner to come out. Buying time would allow them to freeze to death rather than be torn apart like Doc was. Daring to feel the slightest bit of hope, she thought the time might provide a chance for someone to find them and save the day. Tressa knew there wasn't much chance of that happening but it never hurt to hope.

By some miracle that Tressa couldn't see, a noise or movement someplace in the woods along the river caught the creature's attention. It leapt down from the hood and stood sniffing the air then howling like a wolf. The other creatures left their looming positions around the truck and joined what Tressa could only guess had to be the leader of their pack. Todd stopped crying when he finally heard the howls over his sobbing.

"Tressa, did they go away?" Todd asked but Tressa didn't answer because her mind was trying to figure out what was happening and calculate if she could sneak out of the truck, make it over to what was left of Doc's body, and find the keys in his pants, in the bloody pile of what was left of him. Her head darted around, attempting to form a mental picture of where the creatures were. She noted that two were still behind the truck and one was chewing on Doc's remains. Tressa could see the bloody muzzle as it took doc's femur and snapped it in two with one powerful chomp.

"Tressa, I really have to pee." Todd fussed from the back of the truck, sitting up in the seat. "Do you think they will stay here very much longer? I really need to pee bad, Tressa."

"Todd, dump one of the water bottles out and pee in that." Tressa replied.

"I couldn't do that, Tressa! I could never pee in a bottle with you sitting up there so close by with no door or nothing."

"Then pee in your pants, Todd, or don't pee, that is up to you. You can't get out of this truck and I have no idea when or if these things are going to leave." Tressa replied and was sorry for how she had put it to her uncle. Todd couldn't comprehend the danger they were in; he only knew that he had to go. Tressa had taken care of him since her grandparents were consumed by the virus and now he depended on her just like he had depended on them for his whole life. He was forever a child trapped in a very large man's body.

"They look almost like puppies don't they" Todd said having, for a moment, forgotten that he really had to go.

"Yes, just like very big and very mean puppies."

Todd shifted in the back seat so that his head was now looking over the front seat. "They better hope that Zeus doesn't come by here. He won't like them being mean to us at all."

"They are a lot bigger than Zeus. I think Zeus would get hurt if he came by here right now."

Todd howled with laughter causing the creatures to turn their heads toward the truck and Tressa to cringe. "That's funny, Tressa, you're a funny lady! Zeus isn't afraid of anything, not with Perseus with him. They would take care of these bad puppies fast and how."

"OK Todd, you're right, they would handle these guys without a problem. Honey, they are not here so we need to stay quiet remember?" Tressa reminded him.

"I will stay quiet, Tressa." Todd replied. "Tressa, I think I have to pee pretty bad now."

Tressa closed her eyes in exhaustion. Between Todd and the creatures, it was just too hard to keep up with both. "You just need to hold it for a little longer. Can you do that for me? Can you hold it for a little longer when the creatures go away?"

"I can try, Tressa, but I ain't making no promises."

*****

Lori went to Boo's truck and took a quick look inside. Anything worth taking would need to be loaded into the truck that Walter and she would be driving. She looked at the door, stained with frozen blood that coated the handle down to the base. She couldn't tell if that was from the gun shot or from when they were rammed. There was no blood on Virginia's side or in the middle, reassuring her that Virginia and Zeus were not wounded while there. Flipping the seat up, she found a mess of supplies and rags cluttering the small open space. Old Boo always had his rags handy it seemed. "Never could tell when you would need one," he would tell them back at Rivers Crossing, with a wide smile stretched across his wrinkled face. Pulling a few boxes of ammo, she turned to hand them to Walter. She did not find him where he had been. She looked up over the dashboard. Walter was crouched down above the attacker's corpse sniffing his face.

"Walter, what are you doing over there?" Lori asked. Acting like he had not heard Lori, Walter went on with what he was doing. "Come on Walter, leave that body alone. We have work to do before the others come back." Lori could see that he wasn't going to move any time soon so she placed the boxes on the seat and walked over to him. The body's clothes were loose and worn with gaping holes and rips. What had looked like a winter coat was just blankets cut and tied in a fashion as to work as a coat. On one hand there was a girl's pink mitten and the other what could only be the remnants of a leather glove. The fingers were covered in a black dirt substance, much like the face.

The smell was the oddest part to Lori. Judging by his dress and obvious lack of a bath in the recent past she would have thought the odor would be hard to stand even from a few feet away. Instead Lori found his smell to be sweet and hypnotic. Blood rushed through her veins in a rampage, causing her heart to beat so fast she could barely hear anything else. Closing her eyes, Lori lifted her face to the sky and swept her head from left to right taking in the smells and growing drunk on them. The euphoria that was filling her body was too much to handle. Dropping to her knees next to Walter, Lori let out a roar that echoed through the surrounding field and woods. Walter jumped to his feet, backing away from Lori, and let out a growl because all at once he was excited about having a fresh meal and frightened of Lori and what he felt she could do. Snapping her head towards him, she transitioned into a crouching position. Grey lifeless eyes sized up Walter while fangs forced their way from between thin, colorless lips on a cracked, distressed field that made up her face.

Chapter 10

Virginia made her way through the snow as best as she could, trying to stay in Perseus's tracks. Whenever possible she hugged the tree line. It seemed to her that there was less snow underneath the larger branches. Perseus would run so far ahead that she could only see glimpses of black fur for a minute or two and then nothing. After a while he would be charging back toward her, traveling in his usual half-play, half-protection mode. Once assured that Virginia was ok and still following, Perseus would dash off at full speed ahead of her again. Someplace along the way Virginia had missed where the two roads came together in a "T". They were at the very least a mile or so passed where she should have headed back up toward the road. Pain was returning to her leg and the cold was starting affect her. As long as she kept moving there wasn't much chance of her freezing to death, she reassured herself. Looking up at the large flakes falling from the bleak, grey storm clouds above her, Virginia noticed that the wind had died down and the flakes were falling straight down. Her attention was drawn suddenly to the fact she had caught up to Perseus, who was laying low in the snow. As Virginia started to pass him she expected Perseus to leap up and charge forward out in front at any minute. He didn't. Perseus let out a low growl and nipped at Virginia's ankle.

"What's wrong boy?" Virginia asked, looking down at Perseus. He let out a small whimper. She heard it too, howling, and not nearly as far away as she would have hoped. Whatever it was that was making that sound, she knew it had to be something large. Perseus picked himself up out of the snow and started to move forward in front of Virginia. His movements were cautious and looked to Virginia like he was calculating them out in his head. His tail between his legs and every hair on his back standing up made him look larger than he was. Perseus moved forward a few steps at a time. He would stop to sniff the air ahead a few times then take three or for more steps forward. The whole time his face held a silent snarl and his body looked ready to spring into action. Now and then he glanced back to see if Virginia had stayed or was following him into the unknown ahead.

The howls grew louder until Virginia felt that they had to be coming from just beyond the trees. Perseus was now growling and hopping up, slamming his front paws down into the snow, announcing his presence to whatever unseen beasts lay beyond the trees. Reaching into her quill, Virginia loaded an arrow into the cross bow and moved up next to Perseus who again nipped at her. It was an effort to keep his human safely behind him. Virginia paused for barely a second when Perseus stepped through the tree line, out into the open. Following him through with the crossbow raised at the ready, Virginia came out into the open space. There was a truck with what looked like two people sitting in it staring back at her. Between them and the truck were the most grotesque creatures that Virginia had ever seen outside of a movie. Grey bodies with skin clinging, seemingly too tight, covering clearly defined bones and muscle. They were easily double the height of Perseus, who was a larger than normal black lab.

They moved forward toward where Virginia and Perseus. Virginia couldn't imagine how they could walk with claws that looked to be five or six inches long, curved like some kind of knife. The creatures closed half the distance to them and Perseus moved a step closer, showing his teeth and growling in a more ferocious tone than Virginia had ever heard from him before.

The creatures stopped and roared so loud that Virginia and Perseus both too a few steps back. Snarling with its back hunched up, the lead creature took a few steps toward them and the others followed. Virginia drew a bead on the creature's head, hoping that if she dropped it with a clean shot the others would scramble long enough for them to make it to the safety of the truck on the other side of the clearing, or perhaps the cabin. Just as she was going to let the arrow fly, Perseus charged forward three steps causing the creatures to retreat back a few feet. At first Virginia thought there was a chance that they could bluff their way out of this. But all Perseus' show had achieved was backing the creatures up a little and spreading them into a half circle in a wider arc around them. When they started coming forward again Perseus charged several times, trying to force them back. As they grew closer he snapped and snarled at them while they returned the gesture. Keeping Virginia behind him at all times, Perseus seemed to concentrate on the ones that were closer to Virginia and ignored the others who were a few steps farther away. When the distance was such that even Virginia felt that they were too close for comfort she let loose her first arrow, aimed at what she thought was the lead creature. The arrow's point found its mark, nailing him directly between the eyes but bouncing off. There was a slight scratch with a trickle of blood where it had struck. Virginia was scared, if her crossbow was useless there was nothing that she could do to defend herself out in the open. As she judged the distance back into the trees she became aware that the creatures now had almost encircled the two. Perseus had been knocked to the ground dodging a bite from the lead creature and was almost bit in the back by another. Rising up, he charged forward again then dropped back just in front of Virginia. He was snapping like a mad dog at anything around him and his tail was as far between his legs as it could go as he pressed back against Virginia's legs for reassurance that she was still there with him. Feeling something else touch his back, Perseus twisted his head and snapped at it until he saw that it was Virginia's hand. She could feel his heart beating so fast that it seemed like it would explode any minute. Once he knew it was her, he tried his best to melt himself into her legs for protection. Perseus had met his match and the urge to fight or flee was screaming for him to flee. Only Virginia being there kept him steady, he could not leave her there with certain death. His job was to protect her, even if it meant that he would die alongside his beloved human.

The roars and snarling were pierced by a bang. One of the creatures yelped in pain but did not drop. Off behind them more creatures emerged from some place that Virginia could not quite make out. They surged toward the truck, attacking it with more determination than the ones in front of her. *It's as if they are toying with Perseus and I*, she thought. *Playing with us until they grow tired of it and would move in for the kill.* Maybe it was the sight of Perseus or the fact that they had both made a stand. Virginia wondered if no other people or animals had stood their ground against these creatures. Not that it had seemed to do them much good. It looked like this would be their last stand.

*****

Walter felt his human side taking control as the fear grew from the feeling that he might become the fresh meal. Lori had transformed quickly and with such ease that his young mind didn't know what to think next other than he was in serious danger. Lori slid forward, still crouched down like a spring that had been compressed to the point that at any moment it would burst forward. Hand held in front him, Walter tried to bring Lori back to the human side as best he could. "Lori, it's me, Walter, remember the one you were telling about friends and family." She came closer toward him and he tried to shrink in size, showing her that he was no threat to her.

Lori snapped her head towards the sky and then spun facing up the road toward where Charlie and Jermaine had headed to search for Virginia. A gun shot had echoed through the sky forcing her attention off of Walter and to the sounds. Sniffing the air, she could pick up faint, familiar scents. One brought memories of playing along a river bank with a small child, a girl child that she felt a warmth in her chest just seeing. A base drum began to go off in her head the more she remembered. Each *boom, boom, boom* brought a stabbing pain that robbed Lori of all her strength.

Struggle as she did. the result was the same when the last will of her body succumbed to the pounding pain in her head, grasping whatever strength she had left.

"Walter?" Lori uttered barely above a whisper. She felt like her mouth was lined with cotton. A slight pressure pushed against her head and she felt it being lifted, then gently placed down on something soft and warm.

"I am here Lori, you sure scared me there for a while." Walter replied.

'Where are we Walter?"

"By the trucks, we didn't go anyplace." Walter replied. "Did you hear the gun shot?"

"Yes, um no, I don't know what I heard. Was it a gun shot?" Lori replied. "You're shaking Walter, maybe we should get into the truck and warm up a little."

Walter wasn't sure that Lori could get up and he knew that he couldn't pick her up. "We should stay here for a little while. I will go get us a blanket out of Boo's truck."

As he lifted Lori's head up to slide out from underneath of her, Walter could feel Lori's muscles tense as she forced herself up on legs that felt like jelly.

"No, you just help me to the truck and we will rest for a while in the warm cab." Lori said as she tried to walk on her own. Walter pulled the bulk of her weight onto him until he felt like he would buckle under it. Together they slid their feet through the snow to Charlie's truck. Lori fell into the cab and Walter helped her slide up into the seat. With Lori half sitting, half laying in the seat, Walter carefully lifted her legs into the truck and pushed the door closed.

"Walter, do you see the keys?" Lori asked as he closed the passenger door.

"They are right there." Walter replied, pointing at the keys still in the ignition.

Without opening her eyes Loris said. "Turn them towards the front of the truck."

Walter reached over and turned the keys forward and the motor turned over several times without catching. Letting off like he had seen Lori do several times, then turning again, the motor roared to life.

"Now do you see a red and blue line on the dashboard?"

Walter looked until he found the two lines just below the radio. "Found it." He replied.

"Take the lever and move it all the way to the red side, then take the lever next to it and push it to the top."

Walter slid the lever over until the line was a thick red line with barely anything to the blue line. Then he slid the one next to it straight up, causing cold air to gush out. "It is cold air."

"It has to warm up, it will get there." Lori replied. "I am going to rest for a little while. Please watch for anything dangerous." Lori added as she slipped off into a deep sleep.

Chapter 11

It had been a long time since Zeus had run so far without stopping. The snow had been falling steadily but he could still make out the faint tracks to follow. Staying always within those tracks to make the run easier had worked for the first half but Zeus was having a hard time getting enough air into his lungs to keep going. At a spot that looked like either Virginia had sat down or Perseus had laid down, Zeus collapsed onto the ground fighting for air. He wasn't sure he could take another step or if he could even get to his feet again. Panting hard as he tried to catch his breath, a gunshot snapped his head up and once again he rose to his feet using every ounce of strength he could muster. They were close, very close, he could feel it and he had to push on to find Virginia. With aches running rampant over his body, paws feeling like they were walking on pins and needles, Zeus pressed forward toward the last line of trees.

The evergreen branches scraped against the fur on his head as he broke through the line of trees into the clearing. Before him, Perseus backed up against Virginia snapping feverishly at something that Zeus had never seen before. Hair standing on his back, Zeus leapt forward out of the trees and pulled from deep inside of him all the power needed to cross the distance between him and the beasts as fast as he could. The creature nearest Virginia arched its back and moved forward in a plunge towards Perseus's neck for the kill. Zeus kick up snow around him creating a cloud in his wake. As the distance closed he ran harder until he was past the closest creature and smacked into the one going after Perseus. The blood filled his mouth as he clamped down on the creature's neck, knocking it down to the ground, sending up a plume of snow. The creature cried out in pain as it hit. Zeus climbed back up on unsteady legs and started shaking his head back and forth, trying to rip the creatures throat out before it could regain its stance. Instinct told Zeus that he was on top and that he had to stay on top. The creature rolled over, dragging Zeus over top of him. Zeus bit down harder as the full weight of the creature was brought to bear on him. Just as he felt that all was slipping away from him he could hear Perseus growling. It seemed to Zeus to be a long way from him as everything started to fade. Perseus seemed to be coming closer and growing louder and louder. Zeus pushed with his legs until he felt like he could push no more. The creature rolled the other way still within his grasp. Blood was flowing through his mouth in growing volume. As he got to his feet, Perseus had the creatures neck from the other side violently shaking and pulling large chunks of flesh.

Virginia took aim at the next closest creature and let loose an arrow. Blood exploded outward as the arrow found its mark in the creature's eye. It slid to a stop a few feet away from Zeus and Perseus as they left the dead creature and formed up in front of Virginia, facing the other creatures off. Another arrow whizzed over their heads as the sound of a gun boomed again. Two creatures hit the ground and Zeus went after another one that he thought was too close. As more gun shots went off the creatures that were left retreated into the forest. Zeus and Perseus pursued them to the tree line and then stopped, sniffing the air. Once Zeus was sure that they were gone he turned back toward Virginia.

"I told you they would come, Tressa! Didn't I tell you they would come and save us!" Todd screamed with excitement as he ran towards the dogs.

Tressa pointed over towards the road where Charlie and Jermaine had been shooting from. "Looks like you guys all got her just in time."

"We set out to find Zeus and Perseus. Jermaine said. "Plus we figured if we found Virginia we might just as well bring her back too."

Virginia smiled at Jermaine and fake punched his arm.

"I can't tell you how glad I am to see all of you." Tressa added.

"Doc let you guys head out of Rivers Crossing by yourself? That couldn't have gone well." Charlie looked at Tressa.

Hanging her head low she replied, "Doc left town with us, Charlie. He wanted to let you know that he thought you should bring everybody back."

"Where is he, in the truck? Charlie asked. "Did he get hurt?"

Tressa still wasn't looking toward Charlie or Jermaine when she said. "Doc didn't make it, Charlie. The creatures reached into the cabin and pulled him out."

"Where is his body?"

Tressa pointed up past the truck next to the cabin at what looked like a pile of red snow. Charlie walked over slowly with his rifle raised until he came to where what was left of Doc's body rested, scattered. *Why didn't you stay back at the school you crazy old fool?* Turning toward the others, Charlie felt a tear slide down his cheek. Doc had been the only true friend he had ever known. Along with his Annie, Doc made living back in Rivers Crossing bearable.

"What do you want us to do with the remains?" Jermaine asked.

"Snow is too deep and the ground is frozen, no way we could bury him now." Charlie replied. "We can take some of the gas and burn him so that nothing else gets to eat him."

*****

A twitch was moving Lori's right shoulder back and forth repeatedly. Reaching up to rub the muscle she found a hand pushing and pulling her arm. Eyes wide open she slammed herself against the truck door and defensively held out her arm across her body to protect herself. Sitting in the middle of the seat was Walter smiling from ear to ear back at her.

"You scared me, Walter." Lori said as she raised her hands to rub her aching temples. It felt like she had been out on a wild night of drinking back in High School the night before. Visions had filled her head of family, friends, and of horrible scenes of carnage. Scenes that sadly she could not say she was viewing from an outside view.

"There was a lot of gun shots from over that way." Walter said pointing off down the road. "Do you think we should hide until the others get back?"

Lori could see that Walter was trying to hide something from her. Looking back towards the corpse on the street, it looked like the snow had been trampled near it. Maybe even the corpse itself looked like it had been moved. She couldn't tell for sure with her head hurting so bad and the blurry vision that kept creeping in.

Growing impatient for an answer Walter asked. "What do you think we should do? What if it is people who were with that?" He pointed at the corpse but barely looked toward the body.

Lori slid herself behind the wheel and adjusted the seat. Her mind was still somewhat searching its way through a dense fog. She was trying to settle in where there was a reality that she could cling to for just a little while. Reaching up and adjusting the rearview mirror, a faint glimpse of herself peaked at her. A tear slowly slid down a grey cracked face that glowed. Eyes were a solid grey, fog color, like the two-point-zero eyes that had tried to take her life back at the bunker.

Now she knew why Walter was acting strange. *If this was how he reacted when the child was much more like her than the others, how would they react to this?* Lori thought. The previous visions vanished from her head only to be replaced with fear and doubt. Putting the truck into gear, Lori eased it back toward where they had come and to where she could possibly find Charlie. She prayed that her face and body would return to normal by the time she found them.

The going was rough at first with her vision seeming to be clear one moment and so blurred the next that it was hard to tell if they were staying on the road. Walter had moved over hugging the door and had the handle in a death grip.

"What happened earlier?" Lori asked. Walter remained frozen and his gaze fixed out of the side window.

"Did I do something that scared you?" Lori pushed for an answer.

Still Walter remained sitting like a statue.

"Did you eat that man or Boo?" Lori asked with her voice trailing off as she thought of poor Boo frozen under that tree alongside of the road.

"Did I eat them? You are asking me if I ate them?!" Walter replied nearly crossing the distance between them. "I did nothing like that Lori! You said not to hurt family and friends! That is what you said!"

"Then tell me what happened, Walter. I need to know."

Walter returned his gaze to the side window and was silent again. Lori grasped the mirror and studied her face, paying more attention to her mouth and chin then moving down to her shirt. Her teeth seemed to be a little bigger, like she had some kind of fangs. Other than the outward appearance of her skin and the slightly larger teeth there were no signs of blood that she could see. So she didn't eat either of them.

"I don't think I ate them either." Lori said more to herself than to Walter.

"You were going to kill me I think." Walter finally said.

"Oh honey, I would never do that." Lori replied looking at Walter with a feeling of sadness that he would ever think such a thing.

"You say that now but I am not sure you know that when that happens." Walter replied.

"That? What is that?" Lori asked, more confused than she was when her mind was clouded. Walter searched for a way that he could describe what "that" was. "I think that sometimes we turn into like a two-point-zero." Walter stated. "But then we can be ourselves too." He added, looking over to see Lori's reaction.

"I am starting to agree with you on that." Lori replied not quite sure that she did agree but if it would calm Walter down then so be it. Up ahead she could see the RV half on the street and half off in what looked like a clearing. Lori let her foot off the gas pedal and pulled her pistol up checking to see if it was loaded, then took the safety off. Setting it in her lap, she looked over at Walter. "You can lay down in the seat if you want. I don't know what we're going to find up there." Lori explained.

"Should we walk?" Walter asked.

"No, I want to be able to get away fast if we need to." Lori replied as she pressed lightly on the pedal feeling the back end of the truck slide a little to the left as it began to move.

Chapter 12

Charlie saw his truck come to a stop just on the other side of the RV and made his way over to it. He didn't want Lori to see all of the dead creatures before he could fill her in on what they had found and assure her that Virginia and the dogs were safe and sound in good health. As he approached the side of the truck he found Lori and Walter heading toward him. Charlie was struck by Lori's appearance. Their worst fears were materializing and he didn't know what to do. Other than his Annie, no one had made him feel like Lori did with just a smile.

"We heard the gun shots, is everyone ok?" Lori asked, trying to go around Charlie who planted himself directly in her path.

"Everyone is fine here. Well...everyone but Doc is fine." Charlie replied.

"What happened to Doc? Why is he even out here?" Lori asked half knowing what the answer would be.

"Doc is dead. I guess they came out here looking for us." Charlie stated looking away briefly as the point was driven home by saying it out loud. "Some kind of creatures that I have never seen before attacked Doc, Tressa and Todd while they were eating their dinner last night."

"Tressa and Todd?"

"They're fine, more shook up than anything else but I think they will be OK." Charlie replied. "We burned what was left of Doc's body so that they couldn't come back and finish what they started."

"Probably a good idea." Lori replied looking into Charlie eyes and waiting for his reaction to how she looked.

"Jermaine and I were talking about holding up here for the night and bunking everyone down in the RV. It will be crowded, but I think we can all suffer through it for the night." Charlie stated. Lori shook her head no and replied. "I think it will be too crowded and after everything that has happened today we should find a place with enough room to stretch out. A place where if anyone needs to go off alone for a while it wouldn't be outside of the RV."

"That only leaves us with going back to River Crossing or back to Clarksville then. Really the only places that we know for sure that there is a place like that." Charlie replied.

"Clarksville is closer and seems to be the best option." Lori replied. "Walter and I will lead the way."

As Lori turned to go back to the truck Charlie reached out and gently took a hold of her shoulder. Every muscle in her body turned on her and spun to look Charlie in the eye. Knowing what he was going to say or thinking that she knew caused her to fight the urge to start crying. The subject of how she looked would have to be broached, there was no way around it now that Charlie had seen her. Right now was not the moment that Lori could tell him about what had happened. Earlier she had pretended to not know when she prodded Walter for answers. It helped thinking that it had all been a horrible nightmare caused by her exhaustion. The look on Walter's face, the fear that she could smell coming from his body, only served to prove that it wasn't a dream or nightmare. She was turning into whatever "that" was and it scared her as much as it had Walter.

"We need to talk." Charlie stated.

"We do need to, just not here and now, Charlie. Tonight, when we are all together, I will try to explain what I know." Lori replied.

"You lead the way and I will gather everyone else up and follow." Charlie replied. "Go on then and go, that way we don't have to discuss this with the others until we get there." Charlie urged Lori on while she there, looking into his eyes. He knew if the others saw her now they would be there for hours.

Lori swung the truck around as best she could in the snow, until she was faced in the right direction. Charlie went back to the others who had been watching the entire conversation. "Looks like we are going to head back into Clarksville for the night." Charlie said.

"Back to Clarksville?" Jermaine asked.

Shrugging his shoulders Charlie replied. "Seemed like a better option than crowding everyone into the RV and being exposed out here.

"I am not arguing with the plan, just took me by surprise is all." Jermaine replied.

"You mind driving, Jermaine? I have a lot to think about before we get there."

Jermaine shook his head no and replied. "Not at all, you just make yourself comfortable in back someplace and Todd can be my co-pilot back to the barn."

Hearing that Todd's face lit up like it was Christmas morning and he just found a tree full of presents underneath.

"Well let's get going then, been a long, hard day so far and I think I could use a little time to kick back and recharge the batteries."

*****

They slid from the center of the two lane highway until finding traction just before the shoulder. Lurching back toward the center threw everyone riding in the bed a little. For as far as Megan could see to the left or the right a massive herd stood, blocking the road. She knew they would not attack her, believing that was still an issue Megan had problems with. She had walked among them, fed among them, and moved freely without ever being noticed, still she was never comfortable among them. Slowing the truck down to a crawl was making it harder to move through the snow. She kept an eye on as many of them as she could. A voice from alongside her said, "They will not harm you, drive forward, Megan." The warm breath against her neck felt reassuring so she reached up across her body and rested a hand on the face of the voice. She rubbed the hard leathery cheek until she came to the slimy portion and replied. "I know. They still scare me, Bubby."

"He said we would be ok and I think we will be. If you want, I will walk out in front of you until we get passed them." Bubby replied.

"Nah, I got this. You get back in the back and we will head through them."

Pulling forward, Megan built up enough speed so that she could control the truck but not enough to plow through the herd. As if someone had given an order, the herd parted as the truck grew near. Decaying flesh hanging from bone and muscle caused Megan to take a quick glance in the mirror. Her skin looked similar to theirs only she wasn't decaying as far she could see. The smell was the same between them but that was about it. Halfway through a lone figure stood in the middle of the road as the herd was still moving out of the way. It was larger than the others and dressed in all black with a mouth drenched in dried blood as if he had finished eating some unfortunate soul earlier. Megan stopped the truck as she came up to him and the figure walked over to the side of the truck. "I was sure there would be more of you by now." He said to Megan.

"We had a few others but they didn't make it. Once you figure out what's happening to you...it is hard to handle." Megan replied.

"That it is," he replied walking to the back of the truck. "Up ahead there are a few cattle in a corral, go get something to eat and be sure not to let these others in there with you." The Man in Black said.

As the others ran off into the vastness of the herd Megan climbed out of the truck. "You never told me what it is exactly that we are doing."

"Should be fairly easy to figure that out if you think about it."

"I have thought about it and I don't get why I have been picking these people up or why you have been telling them to wait for me." Megan continued.

"Look around you, what do you see, girl?"

Megan took a long look at the creatures standing, decaying all around her. "I see a lot of dead things that are moving when they shouldn't be."

"That is how a human would see them. You're no longer human or have you not figured that part out yet?"

"I am a human that has caught some kind of disease from the plague just like you. Sick, but still very much human." Megan replied.

"Oh there is a little human DNA left in you. But not very much. Look at your skin, your eyes, or your teeth. Ever seen those on a human?"

Megan couldn't argue that, she no longer looked very human or anything like she did when she first met him. "So what am I then, if I am not human?"

"We are new, Megan. We are new. We are the new masters of this world and all that is in it. Evolution decided that the human race had been found lacking. Our world will no longer destroy all that we see, we don't have to. We don't need the things that made us human any longer."

"What about the people that are still alive and not new?" Megan asked.

"Well, some will need to be protected of course. We don't know if we can procreate without them yet. Others will be raised kind of like cattle I suppose."

"Why not just raise cattle?" Megan asked.

The man roared with laughter loud enough to startle the herd. "That's right, you haven't eaten human yet, have you? Cattle is ok when there is nothing else to be found. Much better than that rat you ate in the dumpster. Fresh human now, that is a treat that you will never forget and never want to be without after you have had it."

Megan felt sick to her stomach just thinking about it. "This is why we are here?"

"Not at all. There is a town being set up down south for the new people and we are reaching out to as many as we can find. I guess you could say that we are extending a personal invitation."

"And the other people, the OLD people? What are we doing with them? Rounding them up for the slaughter?" Megan asked.

The man motioned for her to walk with him as he started for the other side of the sea of dead. "We are setting a town up for them across the river from our town. They will be able to live comfortably for as long as they would like."

"Without eating them?" She prodded.

"There will be some kind of tax that they will pay for their safety, of course."

Megan laughed at the term tax. "So they will give you a sacrifice as a tax?"

"Not just me child, they will give us a sacrifice or three to pay for their safety. We really have no idea as of yet how many of us or them are out there."

"None of this seems right to me." She replied.

Just passed the herd a few feet into open space, the Man in Black stopped and faced her with a sad look. "Megan honey, you don't have to journey the same path that we do. Look around you; the world is wide open. You can go wherever you want and do whatever it is that will keep you satisfied. Understand this, and keep it in mind, you no longer look like the humans so they will never accept you as one of them."

Megan walked off toward the corral on her own, leaving him to walk behind her. No longer wanting to debate new or old people, eat or don't eat them, she was going to avoid the conversation or thinking about it for now.

Chapter 13

When they arrived at the barn they found Lori had left the doors open. Jermaine swung the RV around and backed in. Charlie helped him shut and lock the barn doors before he took Tressa and Todd to the lower level. The room was lit up on one side of the room leaving the far side in the shadows. Virginia followed the group in with the Lads, pausing for a few minutes as she recognized the features of Lori sitting in the shadows with Walter. Taking a seat next to Jermaine, she motioned toward Lori and accepted that Jermaine didn't know what was happening either when he shrugged his shoulders. No one was saying anything at all. The room was so silent that Virginia thought she could hear the wind picking up outside.

"Today has been a bad day for us." Lori said breaking the silence.

"Lost some good people today." Jermaine added bowing his head at the thought.

"Boo went down fighting." Virginia said.

"Doc never saw it coming." Tressa sighed and wiped the tear flowing down her cheek.

"They will be missed, they were our friends and our family." Charlie said as he stood up and looked around the room. "I think we should take the night and mourn our losses and then make a new plan tomorrow morning."

"We have to keep following Bob's map." Virginia replied. "Without Bob or his map where would we be right now?" The others all nodded their heads in agreement.

"Doc told Zoe that he would go back for her and the others." Tressa said. "I think we should at the very least send someone back to get them."

"I am not so sure splitting up again would be a good thing." Jermaine replied looking toward Charlie for some back up.

"I am not sure splitting up would work either." Charlie added. "Look what happened today. Virginia, what did happen over there with Boo?"

Virginia closed her eyes so that she could see it all play out in her head. "We were riding along and I was watching down by the river. Boo was telling me the importance of opening up to people and trusting them." Virginia stopped and smiled at the others, fighting back a sniffle and a tear. "When something hit us hard from Boo's side of the truck. He looked like he was hurt and started to tell me to get out of the truck and run. When the truck backed up like it was going to ram us again the motor must have died out. I could see the guy getting out of his truck with a rifle. I guess Boo could too because he forced his door open and took aim. The man shot first and Boo went down." Virginia paused to look around the room, then continued. "Perseus and I were out of the truck by then, taking cover on the other side, when I heard someone coming around the front of the truck. I knew it was OK because Perseus didn't react to the person. It was Boo soaked in blood, his arm looked like it was hanging on by a thread. Well, he used the truck to get another round chambered and told me to take Perseus and run."

"You didn't listen as usual, did you?" Jermaine asked smiling at her.

"He didn't look like he had any fight left in him so I waited until the guy lowered his rifle. He must have thought with Boo down I was easy pickings because he looked pretty surprised right up until the arrow struck his eye." Virginia continued. "I helped Boo down by the tree like he asked me to and then did what he told me to do."

Virginia looked over to Tressa who picked up on the signal. "We were coming to look for you guys and bring you back to Rivers Crossing. It was one of the few times since all of this happening that I felt like a civilized person. We were cooking our dinner over the fire when it grabbed Doc. Todd and I barely made it to the truck. It was then that I noticed that Doc had the keys. Then you guys saved us." Tressa fell quiet.

The room echoed her silence as they all searched inside for a way to grieve their loss. Lori stood up in the shadows and let out a deep sigh. "Something happened to us as well today, while we were waiting by Boo."

Feeling his muscles tighten Jermaine asked. "More of those guys show up?"

"No, no one else showed up, Jermaine. You and Charlie can rest easy about that. For now, any ways." Lori took another deep breath and looked into everyone's face. If this went how she half expected it to go, Lori wanted to be able to remember them all for as long as she could.

"Everyone knows that I have been bitten by a creature." Lori stated.

"Old news, really." Virginia replied rolling her eyes.

"There have been a few changes that followed an episode. I think Doc would call it an episode." Lori said and then waited for their reaction. When no one said anything she continued. "While we were checking out that man who shot Boo…"

"I bet you changed for a minute just like in Rivers Crossing. I bet you did, Lori." Todd said excitedly.

"Todd, let Lori speak." Tressa said to Todd, giving him the shush sign.

Lori's insides were twisting and constricting into knots, muscles were refusing to move as she felt the fear building up and she wanted to run and hide. *Charlie seemed to be ok with the changes that she had gone through today. What about Virginia? Would her reaction be an arrow into her forehead?* Mind was racing at high speed, she took a long, deep breath and stepped out of the shadows into the light. The only sound Lori could hear in the room was her own heartbeat growing louder and faster. *Lub-dub lub-dub*, echoing off the walls back into her face, slapping her cheek with the reality of what was about to happen. All of the possibilities flashed before her as though she was watching some unknown person's life from afar; watching that person make a life or death decision, wondering if they would live to see another day. Zeus rose up with the hair on his back bristling. He sniffed the air, releasing a guttural growl from behind snarling teeth. Slowly he moved forward in a defensive stance, coiled like a spring ready to pop. Lori backed up a step, feeling the inner rage coming to a boil the same way it had when she smelled the sweet flesh of the recently deceased gentleman on the road. Zeus' fear was filling her nostrils, driving the instincts of what she had become. Pain shot through her thighs, her knees hitting the floor with a pop as she fell to the ground. In a soft tone she uttered. "Zeus honey, it's me." She was begging for the dog to stand down and move away, screaming for it inside of her head. Lori could feel the end coming, the final breath of one who had become her trusted companion, her protector, and most of all, he was her and Virginia's friend. Reaching out to him, Lori offered the back of her hand to Zeus to sniff. It was met with several quick snaps and she recoiled. A trickle of blood ran down her wrist from where Zeus had grazed her. The room became a blur with every fiber of Lori's senses zeroing in on Zeus's throat, feeling his heart beat and smelling his fear. Muscles tensed, waiting for the moment to leap and take the dog down. Her brain calculated the distance, speed, and angle need to take Zeus down then turned to sizing up the others in the room. Just as it was ready to move Perseus stepped in front of her and backed up into Lori moving her back. Surprise and shock filled Lori as she moved back recalculating and adding the new threat into her plan. Only this threat was helping her and throwing more confusion into the mix. Confusion that was allowing Lori to take control back. Reaching down she petted Perseus just behind his ear. Zeus saw this and sat down looking at Lori, trying to decide if she was a threat or a friend.

Lori searched their faces, looking for a sign until she locked eyes with Virginia. It was hard enough reading Virginia on a good day, let alone today after what had been shown here. Would she come around like Zeus did? Would it make a difference that the lads were now somewhat OK with her? If need be, Lori could leave the group for their well-being. Leaving her little sister like this would be harder to do.

"So what are you now then?" Virginia asked in a daze.

Lori shook her head as tears began to flow down over the grey, luminescent skin. "I really don't know, Virginia." Raising her head to look away from Virginia she added. "I really could use Doc right about now." Virginia walked over to Lori and hugged her in a way that she had never done before. Not even before the end of times had Virginia ever shown this much emotion. Lori could feel her heart beat against her chest and the wetness from Virginia's tears against her skin. There wasn't the scent of fear, which helped.

"We can leave the group and see if we can find answers." Virginia stated.

"I will go with you guys." Charlie said, looking around.

"I have done pretty good following you, Lori. You promise not to eat me and I am in." Jermaine stated with a hearty chuckle. Everyone looked back at Tressa waiting for her thoughts. "I got no place else to be." Tressa added to the rest of the voices.

"Well then, I think I am going to see if there is any food left in the kitchen that a so-so chef can fix up for dinner." Jermaine said as he headed into the kitchen. Just before he left the room he turned to Lori and asked. "You do still eat the same food we eat, right?"

"Well, if I remember from the trip to Rivers Crossing correctly, I am not one hundred percent sure that we can call what you cook food"

"Jealousy of my abilities will not place you on my good side, missy." Jermaine replied laughing again.

Chapter 14

Megan had taken her shirt off before she entered the corral with the others. They had made fun of her initially but as she was used the snow to clean the cows blood off of her face and chest, many of them could see why she had. Megan didn't want to walk around with dried blood all over her. Her shirt was still clean and she had washed away any remnants of the meal from her body. The Man in Black was talking to another small group. They seemed to hang on his every word like he was some kind of prophet sent to lead them to the promised land. It hadn't been too long ago that she listened in the same manner. The way he had of talking to the group yet making each one feel like he was just talking to them alone…She wondered what he did for a living before the apocalypse. *Probably some kind of used car salesman or con man.* She thought to her own amusement. That was when it had hit her like a slap in the face. This wasn't where she wanted to be and his plans for the future didn't sit well the more she thought about it.

Megan looked around her and saw the town of Clarksville just down the road. He had told her that she could go in any direction she wanted and live any life she wanted. That was what Megan was going to do. Megan walked passed the little group and she could hear the Man in Black speaking. "Hundreds, if not thousands, just like me and just like you, will be coming here tomorrow. That town just a little way up the road will be our first home. A safe place for the new people of the world."

His voice trailed off with each step away from the zombies and the "new people" she took. No one tried to stop her from leaving like she thought they would. Megan could feel their eyes on her until she put enough distance between them to dull the sensation.

Once she came to the edge of town the first thing she saw was a few cars parked in the middle of the street. She checked each for keys and decided that whoever had left the cars must have taken the keys along with them. An odd thing to do, but probably a habit. The first building she took a good look into had been a diner or some kind of restaurant. The door was locked so Megan looked for anything in the cars that could help her pry the door open. Finding nothing in the first car besides a coat that would fit her, she moved onto the second car, or lead car, she thought to herself. There she found a crowbar that she held out in front of her like it was a winning lottery ticket. Smiling from ear to ear, she headed around the front to the diner door. Just in front of the mini-van, her left foot got snagged on something buried beneath the snow. Backing up and using the crowbar to poke and prod at the snow, she was sure that something was down there. Dropping to her knees, she used her free hand to brush the snow back until a pair of frozen eyes were looking back at her. She jumped back and thought about it for a minute. The people from the cars didn't just leave the area, they were helped on their way to a new place off of the earth.

Climbing up from the ground, Megan shrugged off the body in the snow and continued onto the diner door. She felt bad for them but what could she do for them now? She wondered briefly but the answer was absolutely nothing.

At first she thought to use the crowbar to pry the door open. After several attempts to do just that her idea switched to smashing the lower glass of the door.

A twang echoed down the street with the first blow as the crowbar bounced off the glass. That was followed by several quicker twangs before the glass pane shattered from the blows. Looking back behind her she was certain had caught motion in her peripheral vision. She froze, trying to see if there would be more or if she could hear anything. A flash went past her, near the cars on the street. Holding the crowbar in front of her, she slid her feet toward the cars again. A knocking sound came from behind her and Megan whirled around just as a door on the mini-van closed. Backing up against the building she waited for whatever was out there to show itself. When they had decided that they were no longer playing with her, they came out into the open. Their skin was grey but not quite dead looking like the other zombies. Yet not quite like hers either when she took a closer look. They were smart enough to work her into a spot that there was no an easy escape from. Letting the change overcome her, Megan let out a roar meant to scare them off. The creatures roared back at her charging forward to take down their prey. Megan snapped at them like a rabid dog, holding them just far enough away to keep them from biting into her flesh. A long, lone howl caught their attention and they had left her as quick as they had shown up. Megan didn't waste any time getting into the diner. Grabbing a table still covered with dirty dishes from the last meal, she pushed it onto its side and shoved it in front of the broken glass. An old cigarette machine stood guard next to the door. She pushed it against the tables pedestal base.

Sitting down at the bar Megan looked around the room, taking it all in. There wasn't anything fancy behind the bar at all, an old mirror that reminded her of the one in her grandparent's front room flanked by makeshift shelves with bottles of alcohol on them. The tables were vintage, nineteen-fifties era, she thought. Most of the pictures lining the walls were old, faded black and whites with the exception of one. It had an older man and woman standing behind a large cake that said, "Happy Sixtieth Anniversary" in color. For a few seconds Megan felt the weight of her sorrow press against her heart. She could barely remember her mother's face or that of her grandparents anymore. Moving down to one of the tables she laid her head down and fell asleep for a few minutes.

Chapter 15

After Dinner they sat quietly around the table. Even without counting what was happening to Lori and Walter, the day's events left an emotional cloud above them. Doc had been like the father that no one had left since the sickness spread and Boo was that guy that could always be counted on when trouble came knocking. Even Virginia was beginning to think as long as Boo was with her there was nothing to be afraid of. The sudden realization that both of them were now gone weighed heavy on the mood in the room.

"Well, I am going to go up into the barn and double check the doors." Jermaine announced as he rose from the table.

"I think I will come with you, if you don't mind." Charlie asked.

"Not at all. The more the merrier." Jermaine replied smiling.

Following Jermaine up to the barn, Charlie checked the large doors when they got to them. "Ok, you didn't really come up here to check these two doors with me did you?" Jermaine asked.

Charlie smiled then looked down at the floor. "I guess I wanted to get your thoughts on today."

"If you're asking me about Doc and Boo, I think it is a tragedy that will be hard for us to overcome. But that is what we have all been doing all along since this thing started, right? Over coming tragedy at every turn of the road." Jermaine replied.

"That is true, I was asking about…"

"You were asking me about Lori and if I think it is safe?" Jermaine finished for Charlie.

Charlie walked off toward the trucks and rummaged in the glove compartment box until he found a small bottle of whiskey. Offering it to Jermaine first he said, "Yea, I guess that was what I was really asking you."

Jermaine waved off the whiskey. "I would like to but for some reason I think I need to keep my head clear tonight."

"You think somethings going to happen?" Charlie asked.

"I sure hope not, Charlie. Did you see how she was changing right there in front of us, man? I am not too proud to tell you this but I was scared. I was so scared I almost went in my pants, brother."

"I felt the same, Jermaine. She looked like she could take us all out in short order." Charlie replied, taking a long drink from the bottle. "What do you think we should do about it then?"

"What am I going to do about it? I am not doing anything at all until there is a reason to do something about it. As far as I can tell that is still our Lori. The same Lori that followed me into a large herd of zombies to get my wife out. When all hope was lost she stayed there by my side until I decided to go. So No Sir, I am not going to do anything until I know we need to do something!" Jermaine replied reaching for the bottle. "Besides, whether you know it or not, you aren't going to do anything either. You've been making googley eyes at her for over a month now."

Charlie jokingly grabbed his or more correctly Boo's bottle back making a big show of it.

"Awe hell Charlie, if she wanted to do us any harm I think she would have done it by now." He patted Charlie on the back. "Certainly going to make that relationship a little challenging though."

The door opened from the lower level and Lori came up the stairs looking for them. "I thought you guys had enough time to talk about me without me around. The others probably need a little time to take about this too."

"What makes you think that we were up here talking about you?" Charlie asked looking over at Jermaine.

"Yea, that is something that you would think that we have nothing better to discuss than you. Humph." Jermaine replied joking.

"It's ok really." Lori stated. "Believe me if I had someone I could talk to about it besides Walter I would be too."

"Nothing was said bad out here, Lori. You have nothing to be worried about." Charlie replied handing her the bottle. Lori declined. "I am not sure how the other would react to alcohol. Might not be a good thing you know." Charlie and Jermaine nodded their heads in agreement.

"I think Walter and I should go check the house out." Lori said.

"We can check it out in the morning, with the dogs." Charlie replied.

"I think Walter and I should check it out tonight and then we should sleep in it." Lori added.

"What do you mean sleep in it?" Charlie asked. "We should all stay in the barn and the bunker below."

"I think for now we would all sleep better if we were out there, Charlie." Lori said.

"Ok, I see what you're driving at, Lori." Jermaine said agreeing and then continued. "But I think Charlie and I would feel better with you in the barn. You can sleep in the RV and if it makes you feel better we will lock the bunker door."

Charlie shook his head no in a dramatic fashion to show his disagreement.

"Charlie, it is what Jermaine just said or in the old farm house. You decide what makes you feel better and I will do it."

"I guess in the barn if we have to do it that way. I am not liking this one little bit though." Charlie replied.

"Charlie, after my family died and then old Bob, all I had left in this world was Virginia and the lads. Then I met you when we got to Rivers Crossing and I fell in love with you. I can't sleep in the bunker not knowing if I will change or what will cause me to change." Lori said with tears running down her cheeks. Jermaine pushed Charlie forward and Lori wrapped her arms around him burying her head into his chest.

"I will sleep out here too then." Charlie said into Loris hair as he kissed her head. Lori broke away. "No, you will stay in the bunker with the others, Charlie. Trust me, I am not even sure that Walter feels safe being out here but I know that I feel it is better for you guys that he is."

"OK, OK we will do it your way." Charlie relented.

"I keep trying to tell him that life is easier if he would just learn to go along with what you want." Jermaine said mocking Charlie. "Now that the sleeping arrangements have been agreed on, what are we planning for the next couple of days?"

"We need to keep following the map." Charlie replied.

"Someone needs to go get Zoe and anyone else that wants to leave Rivers Crossing." Lori said.

"How do you think they are going to react when they see you?"

"They're not going to see me until they get back here." Lori replied.

"You can't possibly be talking about splitting up again?" Charlie was shaking his head again.

"We have the barn and the bunker, those of us that stay here will be safe until you get back." Lori said.

Eyes darting to Jermaine and then back to Lori again and again, Charlie asked. "I am going by myself to get her and the others?"

"Of course not, Jermaine will go with you in the truck. I am sure one of the buses still run for the ride back." Lori replied smiling.

"Why do I need to go?" Jermaine asked joking then answered for himself. "I know, my job is to keep your Charlie safe and lend a calmer perspective to the venture."

Chapter 16

A barrage of knocks followed by brief silence and then a more intense barrage of knocks on the window pane, woke Megan up. Through sleepy eyes she was shocked at the sight outside of the diner. People were walking up and down the street. A few were pushing the mini-van and car from the center of the road while others were digging up the frozen bodies. In the middle of it all, blocking her view of more, was the Man in Black. He had been the offending knocker that, with his annoying pounding, had dragged her from a beautiful dream back home with her family.

He pointed toward the door and rotated his hand in an unlocking motion until Megan nodded in understanding. She moved the cigarette machine out of the way, then dragged the table back to its original position. She paused before twisting the knob to unlock what was left of the glass door. Glass crunched beneath his boots as he entered and brushed passed Megan, picking up the crowbar from the bar where she had left it. In one fluid motion he lunged toward Megan and she felt the swoosh of the crowbar passing by her face. Just missing her head, it landed with a crash against the cigarette machine. "These things are as good as having gold nowadays" he said grabbing a pack. "You can take a few as your finder's fee." Roaring with laughter from his own wittiness, the man sat at the very table Megan had been sleeping at.

"I take it you have decided to stay?" he asked her.

She sat at the bar, swinging the barstool around so she could look at him. "I stayed here last night to get out of the cold."

He swung the crowbar in an arch across the table, carving a deep, loud scratch until reaching the edge. Lifting it up a few inches he then let it drop to the table with a bam. "I kinda figured you would go back down south to your little dumpster." Scratch...... Bam. "I know you just can't wait to dine on rats again." Scratch......Bam. "Instead, you went north." Scratch.....Bam. "Right where I said we were all going to meet up with others like us." Scratch......Bam.

"I went where I saw buildings that I could wait out the night in. Nothing more, nothing less." She replied, "What is it you're trying to do here? Who made you king of the freak show?"

The man let the crowbar slam down on the table one more time with a louder bang. "King of the freak show? Child, this is not my show at all. We are a movement of the new and improved." He shook his head in disbelief at how dense she was seeming. "A group of us were struggling with what it was that we have become. We walk among the dead without being attacked. We fight the urge to eat other survivors...even when their scent becomes so enticing..."

Megan interrupted him. "Then who is in charge of all of this?"

"We have elders. They vote on decisions. They decide what is the best way for us to survive and thrive in our world."

119

He replied in a matter of fact way that made Megan feel stupid for a moment. "Then why here? Why out in the middle of cornfields, far from anything else?"

"This is just a starting point. You could say that this is where we can experiment and see just what works and what doesn't work." The man replied.

Megan slowly turned the barstool back and forth, trying to judge if she was being misled.

"Last night something came after me." Megan said looking into his face, trying to read his expression. "It was like they were hunting me."

"Regs?" he asked.

"I don't know what Regs are." She replied.

Smiling back at her, he responded. "Regs are regular people. Nothing like you and I."

"No, they were not Regs." Megan replied, stressing the word Regs. "They were like us… but not like us; kind of a cross between the stiffs walking around and us."

"Oh, you saw some of the mutes last night then." He replied waiting for her reaction, then continued. "They are mutations from the first strain I think. They didn't quite make it as far along as us. We think that they see us as humans or to put it plainly, they see us as food."

"What a messed up word we have now."

"I guess that depends on how you see it, Megan. We have been talking for a while now and neither of us has pulled out a cell phone to "check in" or look up this restaurant. Neither of us texted anyone. I call that progress." The man replied, smiling from ear to ear.

"Anything else out there that I should know about?" Megan asked.

"The virus has mutated in more ways than I or anyone else could possibly tell you about. Like I said before, it is a whole new world out there."

"Something was howling last night that drove them away." Megan said.

"Animal mutations of the virus. Huge dog looking creatures. Beautiful and horrifying at the same time I think." He replied.

She hopped down off the stool and held her hand out to the man. "Well, it has been nice meeting you and thank you for all you have done for me. I never did catch your name though." Shaking Megan's hand, a little more vigorously than she expected, he replied, "Stay safe, child. And try to keep your distance from the Regs and Mutes."

Noticing how he completely went passed giving his name to her Megan nodded in agreement and picked up her stuff from the table. Holding up the crowbar like he was going to hit her, he flipped it over, presenting the handle to her. "Take this and the gun I gave you." Taking the crowbar, Megan slid it into her backpack and left the diner.

******

The room was dark and scary. Only the faint glow and hum from the heater was there to guide Todd through the room. It didn't do much to prevent him from bumping into the furniture. He groped his way toward where he thought the stairs leading up into the barn were. Having looked all around for the puppies, Todd knew the last place that they could be at was the barn. The sounds of the air filtration backed up by odd noises coming from the freezer and refrigerator were almost too much for Todd to handle. Several times he stopped and thought about going back to the safety of his sleeping bag on the floor next to the bed where Tressa was sound asleep . The lure of playing with the puppies was just too strong to be denied. Listening for each new sound that mixed in with the others, Todd moved forward. The stairs proved to be much harder to climb in the dark and on more than one occasion Todd fell, slamming his knees into the steps above him. Making like a statue, he would freeze and listen for signs of Tressa coming to find him where he shouldn't be. Once he felt that no one was coming he would stand on shaky legs and feel his way up the next step.

At the top of the stairs Todd came to the door. When he had decided to look for the puppies in the barn, he had no idea that the door would be closed and locked. It had never been locked when he came or left before. Grasping the handle and turning with all his might until he felt pain in his hand, he stopped and tried to remember what the door looked like in the light. Sliding his free hand all over the door, he found a latch and twisted it. A loud click seemed to echo down the stairs so he froze and listened for Tressa again. Convinced that no one else had heard it, he reached for the knob again. Still it would not move so he once again put all of his might behind it until his hand started to ache. Sitting on the step he thought to himself, *come on Todd, how do big boy's open doors? You're a big boy so you can open this door. Yes, you are Todd, you're a big boy and you can do this.* Once again he gripped the door and twisted it as hard as he could. That was when Todd noticed a bump on the handle, pushing into the palm of his hand. His large fingers found it hard to manipulate the small bump. After a few minutes of trying and nearly breaking down into tears, the bump moved to the right with another click. He stepped back and almost fell down the stairs in his excitement. Reaching forward again he twisted the knob and the door popped open with a twang.

Once in the barn Todd forgot all about the puppies as his eyes tried to adjust to the room. There was a light on in the RV and a slight glow shining down on him from the steps above. The stairway leading up to the top was bathed in the glow, making the decision to go up them easy for him. He climbed them as fast as he could, not bothering to care how much noise he made. He knew that Tressa had really good ears but he didn't think she could hear this far away.

At the top he found a long thin walkway suspended from the roof leading from one side of the building to the other. On either side of the walkway were large windows that let him see for miles and miles. "This is just like back at the other town when I was up on top with Mr. Charlie." Todd told himself, then looked around to see if anyone had heard him. Satisfied that no one had heard him he looked out the window on his left side. The only thing out there was the house next to the barn. Losing interest quickly he moved further down the walkway and pressed his nose against the glass on the right side. Pausing to laugh for a moment because his breath had fogged the glass up he then moved a little further down and looked out into the night sky. There he saw lights of all sizes and shapes coming from the town. Cars were driving all over the place, some stopped and some just kept driving around. Patterns had always fascinated Todd since he was a little boy. Making heads or tails out of everyday things in life was far beyond his abilities but he could look at a pattern and see it for what it was and what it meant. The lights were moving randomly, there was no real pattern to see there. He ignored them as best he could. Between the lights and where Todd was watching from atop of the barn there were two patterns moving through the darkness. Barely visible to him, Todd could nonetheless make them out. They were moving with purpose and that captured Todd's attention. One group moved around the lights, just off far enough away to stay in the dark. First one would move and then the rest would follow. It was like they were playing a game of follow the leader. Not far behind that pattern was the other pattern. It was moving back and forth behind the first pattern like it was looking for the first group. Todd's brain was busy calculating when the second pattern would overcome the first pattern that he missed the sound of footsteps coming up the stairs behind him. Just as he had picked the spot where the second pattern would meet the first pattern a voice behind him said.

"You found it hard to sleep too?" Todd jumped so high that he cracked his forehead against the window sending a shudder through the pane. Grabbing his aching head he turned to find Virginia and the lads standing there looking at him.

"Don't worry, Todd. I couldn't sleep either. Your secret is safe with me." Virginia said, trying to settle him down. "See anything interesting out there?"

Todd lowered a hand from his forehead and wiped away the tears that formed the instant he had hit the glass and pointed out the window. Virginia looked on and saw the lights moving all around the town too.

"A lot of lights out there, Todd." Virginia said acknowledging what Todd was pointing at.

Todd shook his head no and pointed again out the window. "The lights are boring, Virginia. They don't have any reason to why they move." Pointing again he tapped his big finger on the glass. "See those over there? There are two groups in the dark."

Virginia strained her eyes until she could just barely make out the two groups. "What do you think they are up to?" She was asking herself more than she was asking Todd but that made no difference to him.

"That one is trying to catch that one." Todd offered. "They will catch them just over there by the end of that street Virginia."

At times like this Virginia thought she was getting a glimpse of the man Todd could have been had life not thrown him a curveball. Serious, calm, and most of all focused. He was studying the two groups as they moved across the field. One time he had told Virginia that it was easy to do if she tried. "How do you know they will meet over there?" Virginia asked Todd knowing the answer he would say even before he did.

"It is easy Virginia, just look at them and look at the lines. Do you see the lines?" Todd replied. Jabbing the window with his finger Todd traced out a path that group two would take. Sure enough they zigged where Todd said they would and zagged right where he said they would zag. "You see it now Virginia? Do you see it?" Todd asked, growing impatient with her.

"Yes, Todd I see it." Virginia replied. "We should go get some rest so that we can tell everyone what you found in the morning."

Todd looked down at his shoes and started swaying. "Do we have to tell them Virginia?"

"I think we have to, don't you?"

"Tressa will not be happy with me opening the door and coming up here without her saying that I could." He said looking at Virginia then back down at his shoes.

"How about I tell Tressa that I accidentally left the door open?" Virginia asked.

Todd jumped up and raised his hands above his head. "Would you do that Virginia? Would you really do that for me?"

"Just this once I will. Next time you should ask Tressa before you sneak out like this."

"I promise never-ever to do that again! Thank you Virginia, thank you very much." He yelled over his

126

shoulder as he ran down the stairs to get back in to his sleeping bag before Tressa noticed he had left.

Chapter 17

Outside of the diner people were busy settling into Clarksville. The sun was out. Temperatures were threatening to reach fifty degrees Fahrenheit. A heavy set guy was using an old coal scoop to shovel the wet, heavy, melting snow off the sidewalk to the house he claimed for his family. If not for the zombies moving freely around the street, Megan would have thought she had been transported back in time to the days before the apocalypse. Faces without names smiled and waved at her while others bid her a good morning. At first she just walked by, acting as if they did not exist. After a while she started to smile or wave back. The Man in Black was right about one thing: it felt good to be a part of a group again, a community of people just like her.

Stopping in front of some kind of dollar store or maybe a general store, she watched as the new owners made themselves at home amongst the t-shirts and candles that covered almost every available space.

Further down the street she came to what she guessed was an old car dealership. It wasn't large and sprawling like the ones back where she was from. It was large enough to have maybe twenty cars outside in the lot, with perhaps five or ten inside of the showroom. The crowd around it was growing quickly while it looked like the old showroom was packed full. Pushing her way through the crowd Megan was about half way when she started to notice more zombies than people milling around the lot. That didn't make a lot of sense to her, they couldn't drive, and she doubted that they could even remember what a car was for. That was when she saw the first one standing inside the lot. Its eyes were sunken deep, with a lost look on its face. It moved more by instinct than actually thinking where it was or what it was doing. The look was shared by every face inside the lot. In the showroom there was no one above the age of thirteen. They were packed in there like sardines in a can, faces pressed against the glass looking out. Moving further in, Megan tried to get up next to the lot so that she could get a better look.

She placed her hand on the back of someone in front of her to give them a gentle nudge out of her way. Megan felt the skin underneath the Cubs' shirt slide right off their back. Snapping her hand back and nearly vomiting, she moved around the dead creature, as it hissed at her.

It hit Megan as though someone had kicked her in the face. The people in the old car lot weren't like her or the others at all. The Man in Black had lied to her, again, about what was going on. She knew she should have figured it all out from the things that he had told her and the group all along. It looked to her like hundreds of "New" people. as he had called them, where her trying to start a new life or something that resembled a life. The people in the car lot were not there for that, they were the "cattle" that he had spoken of. At the time she had thought that there was a chance that he was over stating that portion of his story, to get her back in line. Seeing it with her own eyes brought it all home.

Anger was building up inside of Megan to the point of overcoming her. Looking to the left she saw the dead mingling freely with the zombies and the dog creatures, on leashes, held by large men with the same skin she had. To the left there was more of the same, most looked like they were at their favorite sandwich shop waiting for the doors to open and let them in for a quick and tasty meal. Pushing her way back out of the crowd and breaking free onto the street, she felt tears start to flow. She started making her way out of town. She didn't smile back at anyone or wave from that moment forward. She didn't know what she was—or what they were for sure. She did know that no matter what they were, they had all been changed into monsters; more evil and horrifying to her than any she had ever seen in a horror movie.

Megan broke into a run as fast as she could carry herself to get away. The sounds and smells of the area soon began to grow fainter. She came to a cross street that had only faint signs of tire tracks with a few footsteps. Stopping and looking around, she didn't see any signs that anyone had been down the street recently. Turning and walking inside the tire tracks, she moved as fast as she could for about two hundred feet, while the town grew smaller behind her. Up the road she could see a barn and what looked like an old farm house. *Good enough spot to stay the night*, she thought. She could spend the rest of the day trying to make heads or tails out of what she had just seen.

*****

Zeus laid his head down in Virginia's lap and stared up at her through big eyes. Virginia knew just what he wanted and took her hand, stroking him from just behind the ears down to his collar. She watched as Zeus closed his eyes and settled in for all the attention he could get from her. Each time she would start at the top of his head Zeus would press down on her lap and let out a sigh of relief. She loved watching the dogs and how the interacted with her. Never having really understood people that well, the dogs were a welcome change. They loved her for what she was and Virginia loved them for what they were. She would give her life to keep the lads safe and they had laid down their lives for her too many times for her to count. Zeus' face was no longer jet black like Perseus'. It surprised Virginia to see just how white his muzzle had become at the tip, leading back to a grayish color.

Perseus came over and slammed his body into Virginia's side as he sat next to her, causing Zeus to give him a quick growl for invading what Zeus saw as his time.

The door below opened and Jermaine and Charlie came up into the stall where Virginia and the lads were sitting on the ground in the hay.

"I wondered where you got off to, we missed you during breakfast." Jermaine said, looking down on them as he topped the stairs and stepped into the stall.

"I asked Lori if you or one of the dogs could ride with us and she said that she thought it would be better if you stayed." Charlie stated before Virginia could offer to go.

"You know how Lori is, Charlie." Virginia replied.

"Yes, we do know how she is." Jermaine added with a slight laugh.

Virginia moved Zeus's head off of her lap and stood up, much to his displeasure. "I think there is something that you both need to see before you go." Virginia said motioning for them to follow her. Leading the way, Virginia took them up to the walkway at the top of the barn. Once up there, Jermaine slowed down stepping out onto the walk way and placing his hand on one of the cables it was suspended from. He could feel a slight vibration with every step that Charlie and Virginia took. Looking over the side, it was a long way down to the barn floor. Jermaine closed his eyes for a second and he could feel the whole walkway move with their steps and part of him wanted to turn and go back down the stairs. When Zeus and Perseus barreled past him, knocking him to the side, Jermaine thought for sure he was going over.

"Are we sure this will hold all of us?" Jermaine asked.

"I guess we will find out if we get down faster than we came up." Charlie replied joking with him.

"We need to work on your sense of humor, that's what we need to do." Jermaine said as he started to move where Virginia and Charlie were standing. "Maybe the dogs could wait over there so we are spreading the weight out a little. Or better yet, send them downstairs."

Virginia handed Charlie the binoculars from the truck and pointed towards town. "You might want to have a look before you think about leaving today."

Charlie took them and focused in on the town. "Damn! There are people all over the place." Charlie said handing them to Jermaine.

"Not just people, have a look over by the old, beat up truck in the back yard." Jermaine replied.

Charlie looked where Jermaine was point and he could just make out something moving around. "The one with no tires?"

"Yes, that's the one. Now pan toward the right from there." Jermaine replied.

Charlie eased his way from the truck over to the right of it. "What the hell?" He eased over toward the parts of the main street that he could see through the houses. "Here, look straight up that third street from the left of the truck." Charlie said as he handed the binoculars back to Jermaine.

Following Charlie's directions, he moved to the left and then slowly up the street until he could see Main Street. Lowering the binoculars to his chest Jermaine was silent for a few seconds as he tried to gather his thought. "It can't be." It was all he could come up with as he looked from Virginia to Charlie waiting for some idea they might have had with what was happening out there.

No one said a word until Charlie broke the silence. "I think this will change our plans a little. We should talk about this with the others."

"What is that over there?" Virginia asked pointing at the street in front of the farm.

Jermaine zoomed in on the figure walking up the middle of the road with the binoculars. "Looks like a woman. Maybe from the town?"

"Great!" Charlie raced down the stairs, pushing past Jermaine so fast that it knocked him off of balance. The lads caught up to Charlie first at the bottom of the stairs, followed by Jermaine.

Trying to catch his breath he asked, "What was that all about?"

Charlie pointed over at the door. "I wanted to make sure the big door was closed. We don't know what we're dealing with out there yet." Moving over to the RV, Charlie banged on the side several times and shouted. "Anyone awake in there yet?"

"How could anyone still be asleep with you and Jermaine running up and down those metal stairs?" Lori answered from inside as she opened the door.

"Just a lone person coming down the street?" Lori asked.

"As far as we can tell." Jermaine replied.

"Virginia, I think the lads could use a little exercise." Lori said to everyone's surprise.

Charlie shook his head and blocked the way in front of Virginia. "I think Jermaine or I, maybe both of us should go check her out."

"Then they would know we have two large guys in here who could put up a fight. If they see Virginia coming down the street it might keep the tension to a minimum." Lori said.

"Until they get to know her and the dogs...they will be wishing that Charlie and I came out to meet them then." Jermaine said laughing.

Placing her hand on the back of Virginia's shoulder, Lori led her to the large doors and started unlocking them. "Just take it nice and slow, Virginia. If she looks like me...try not to show any fear or aggression. I can smell that and so will she." Lori stated.

Chapter 18

Sliding the door open let the sun wash across Virginia's face, blinding her for a few seconds. Looking back into the shadows, she could feel the others standing there watching her every move. As she started to drag the door closed Lori said, "Leave it open so we can see you from here."

Virginia smiled into the emptiness and turned to catch up with the dogs. As was the custom, Zeus stayed close by right in front of Virginia while Perseus charged ahead. He didn't go as far as he would have in the past. Something changed in Perseus the day they found Todd and Tressa by the river. It was warmer than it had been for a while and Virginia liked the feel of it. Her feet sloshed through the melting snow and the sounds of falling water off of the old house and barn were pleasant to listen to. At the street she turned left with the dogs and prepared to confront the stranger. Picking up the pace a little Virginia cradled the crossbow against her chest with an arrow loaded and ready to fire. Zeus was studying the figure walking toward them looking for signs of danger. At a distance of twenty feet from the stranger Virginia stopped and looked her over. Gray, coarse skin peaked out from the hoody as the person stopped, facing Virginia. "I haven't seen too many dogs these days."

"They are out there, if you look." Virginia replied.

"Are you alone out here?"

"I have my dogs." Virginia replied, widening her stance in case she need to fire the arrow.

Throwing the hoody off of her head, Meagan stepped forward until both Zeus and Perseus growled. "I don't mean anyone here any harm. We have to get out of here, this place is no longer safe."

"Seems pretty safe at the moment." Virginia replied.

"Ok, Ok. Let's start over and see how it goes. My Name is Megan and I just left that town over there. You are?"

Virginia looked toward the town and could see people moving around. If she could see them then if anyone happened to look they would see her. "I am Virginia, let's move up by the house and talk there. Wouldn't want whatever has you so spooked to see us out here in the middle of the road."

Megan shook her head in agreement and started to walk when Zeus growled again, rising up. "Zeus and Perseus, lets go." Virginia commanded and Perseus took the lead with Zeus staying in between Megan and Virginia.

"You're not afraid of me?" Megan asked leaning up against the house.

"Not really." Virginia replied as the barn door slid further open and Lori and Walter came out. "I guess not, looks like you have met a few of us already" Megan said.

"Hi, my name is Lori and you have met my sister, Virginia." Lori walked up, joining them.

"Now I know why you didn't lose it when you saw me." Megan said to Virginia. "As I told your sister here, my name is Megan and I just came from that town up the street. We need to get away from here as fast and far as we can."

"We saw the people in town from one of the barn's windows." Lori replied

"I don't think that you can see the real people from here but you can see people like you and I." Megan replied.

"Real people?" Lori asked

"Why don't we all go into the barn where we can sit down and talk where it is a little warmer." Charlie offered as he came up. Megan sized him up and could tell he was human. "I could sure use a good cup of coffee, if you have it." Megan replied

"Good idea, Charles," Lori stated then added. "Why don't you guys go ahead and Megan and I will be right along."

Virginia and Charlie looked at each other, trying to figure out what Lori was up to then turned and started walking to the barn. Charlie waved his hands in front of him to let Jermaine know that all was good and they were coming in.

"Come inside, have a cup of coffee and get warmed up. Let's hear what it is you have to say and then we will decide on what happens next." Lori said to Megan.

"Like I told your sister, I don't mean anyone here any harm. I saw the tire tracks and wanted to warn you is all." Megan replied.

Moving in close to Megan, Lori let the beast lose for just an instant. Just long enough for a growl from deep within her to escape. Megan froze mid step and wanted to run as fast as she could. Never had she seen anyone do what Lori did; to change so quickly into and back out, like blinking her eyes.

"You see, I know you will do no harm, Megan. What you need to remember is that if I don't believe what you have to say is true or that you are setting us up in any way....well, it will no go well for you, you understand me?" Lori asked.

Megan shook her head yes and followed Lori into the barn. The smack of the doors closing behind her caused her body to tense and jump.

Charlie began showing Megan the way to the bunker when Lori stepped in front of him. "I think coffee would be good up here where we all have a bit more room to move around. You know how I like mine, Megan?"

"Black is fine, no sugar or cream." Megan replied.

Confused at staying up in the barn, Charlie rolled his eyes. "Do you have a preference too, as long as I am playing waiter that is?"

Jermaine smiled at him and said, "I think I will come with you and get mine. You're a little heavy on the sugar."

Lori led Megan over to a work bench along the wall. From the looks of it she knew that Old Bob had no hand in building it. It looked sturdy enough to do paper work or read the morning paper, not much else. It didn't have the finished feel that Bob embed into everything he made.

"I am only here to let you know what is going on in town." Megan stated.

"And what is going on down in town?" Lori prodded Megan.

Megan looked into Lori's eyes, trying to decide just how far she should go with the story. She was not one hundred percent sure that in the end, Lori wouldn't kill her anyway. "I met a man a while back that helped me understand what I am, what we are. I followed his directions until we came to this place, Clarksville."

"What is it that you are?" Lori asked.

"I'm not completely sure how I should answer that. I suppose you could say that I, like you ,am one of the 'new people;' a cross between human and the creatures."

"So you were bitten?"

Meagan looked back her with a 'no duh,' look on her face.

"And these 'new' people you were with, what is their deal?" Lori said.

"I found out that their plan is to create a new world with people like us. The word I got was they would set up a town on one side of the river for us, and another one across the river for regular people." Megan continued.

"Then we would all live together like one big happy family?" Lori asked.

"In a way, there would be a cost to the regular people to have safety, to be able to have a life." Megan replied.

Lori thought for a minute until it dawned on her what Megan was talking about. "You were ok with this plan?" Lori asked.

"Yes…and no. I loved the idea of getting back to some kind of normal. To be honest, I was a little excited when I saw everyone in town, working to clean up and make it a real, live town again." Megan replied. "Then I saw the people and I knew it was all or most of it was a lie."

"Tell me about the people." Lori demanded.

"The Man in Black, the one who found me, who was in charge, he had talked about cattle a lot. How people would be somewhat like cattle in the new world." Megan cut her reply short, hoping Lori would put two and two together without her having to spell it all out.

"Where are the people? Are they settling in like the rest?" Lori asked.

Ashamed of what she was about to say and a little scared of Lori, Megan tried to change the subject when Charlie and Jermaine returned. "Thank you, I haven't had a good cup of coffee in a long time."

"Don't go expecting it to be good, he made this pot." Jermaine replied.

"People!" Lori demanded.

"They are all being kept in this old car lot; children in the showroom and all of the rest in the lot." Megan blurted out.

"We will need to go have a look before we go to Rivers Crossing." Jermaine looked at Charlie.

"Maybe on the way out of town we can drive through and act like we are looking for supplies." Charlie replied.

"You can't go there! You two will stick out like a sore thumb. I can smell you're human— so they can too." Megan said.

"What if we stay in the truck and make a slow pass?" Charlie asked.

"I think that would make you stick out even more." Lori replied. "I will go into town and maybe take Walter with me."

"I can go with you if you want and take you right to the people." Megan offered.

Lori looked into Megan's face for any hint that it was a trap. The smell of fear was heavy on the girl and Lori doubted that it was all fear of her.

Charlie took the last of his coffee and finished it. In truth he had to admit that Jermaine was right about his coffee. It left a lot to be desired in the world of good coffee. "So then Jermaine and I will just stick to our original plan?" Charlie asked.

"You can't!" Megan stated. "If they see you leaving it will draw them here to us."

"Then we will leave after dark, head off in the other direction and work our way back over to the highway." Charlie replied.

"You guys don't understand, and I don't know how to tell you so that you will!" Megan yelled looking from face to face.

"Then try as best you can." Lori said, reaching out placing her hand on top of Megan's.

"There are other things, other creatures out there. Animals have been touched by the plague. The ones that I saw are huge, hideous looking creatures; kind of a cross between a bear, dog, and some kind of big cat. Then add in something out of a museum of prehistoric animals and you have exactly what it was that I saw." Megan paused waiting for them to get the picture in their minds. "Then there is something like us but not like us."

"Two-point-zeros." Virginia said. "They are like zombies, only smarter and faster?"

"Yes! Yes, that is exactly what they seem to be like. Only, they do not like us, the Man in Black said they see us as humans."

"If you take the truck one of the lads could ride with you. Run into any problems and you would have a little help." Virginia added.

"Might make you stick out more." Jermaine added.

"No, we follow the same route that Megan took to come here." Lori replied. "You up for a walk, Walter?"

Walter smiled and shook his head yes at the thought of getting away from all the sweet smells that hung, tormenting him, in the barn.

"Ok then, it is decided, Walter, Megan and I will go see what is happening while the rest of you start getting ready to leave. Once we are back we will wait for night and then get as far away from here as we can." Lori stated.

****

Chapter 19

Her fingers were beginning to sting and her feet no longer had any feelings in them at all. The nearest person to Zoe had given up all hope and seemed resigned to accepting his fate for what it was. She didn't recognize his face so that meant that he probably wasn't from Rivers Crossing. Earlier he had given away his coat and shoes to another person like Zoe that had been dragged out in the middle of the night from a sound sleep. In the first few hours after being herded off the bus into the lot, Zoe had tried to move around as much as possible in hopes of running into Doc and Tressa. Once the cold had settled into her bones she stayed in a spot that looked to her like everyone would eventually walk passed. Now no one was moving around to stay warm, including her. The edge of the lot seemed to offer more hope of escape while the center offered more warmth from all of the body heat. Zoe was somewhere in between there, slowly feeling her body begin to shut down. Her eyes were heavy and fighting off the urge to close them was growing harder when movement cause the crowd to shift like a wave. Screams pierced the air and then the wave surged back to where it had started, followed by silence.

"I have a knife," said a voice dressed in a pair of shorts and a tattered old tank top. Zoe wondered if he had been dragged from bed like her or if he from a warmer place. In the end she knew it didn't really matter very much. "That is good for you, Mister." Zoe forced herself to reply.

"I will give it to you if you will slit my throat for me." He stated looking at her through dead eyes.

'I don't believe that I can raise my arms up." Zoe replied.

"Do you want me to slit yours before I find someone to do mine?" he asked.

"No need, I don't feel like I can hold out much longer." Zoe replied. "I am going to join my nephews soon."

The man suddenly fell silent as he thought about his wife and children. Try as he did he could no longer remember their faces. "It will be good to see family again." He mumbled as he moved back into the crowd.

Zoe forced her legs toward a thicker part of the crowd, moving as near to the center of a group as she could. Feeling the warmth from the others around her, she closed her eyes letting their bodies keep her upright. It wasn't too long before the crowd began moving again as people on the outside pushed to get into the center. Cries screamed out again from both sides of Zoe. She looked around, trying to see where they were coming from. Like a magnet being pulled to metal, she felt her legs begin to move forward against the flow. Squeezing where she could, pushing and shoving in other places, until they seemed to part for her. The muffled cries behind her grew faint as the ones in front grew more desperate. The further she moved the more desperate the flow was to get passed her. Hands that she could not see grabbed and moved her around them into the more unseen hands until she reached the outside of the crowd on the edge of the lot. Everything and everyone was covered in a blackish red substance that she knew had to be blood. *Where was all this blood coming from?* Zoe thought to herself as she tried to take everything in before her. People stood just outside of the lot looking in and pointing at the people inside. At least, she thought they were people. Worn down from the cold and exhaustion she couldn't be completely sure if what she was seeing was really there. Their skin didn't look normal to her. The urge to move closer grew inside of her because she needed to know. She moved passed a small woman trying desperately to wipe away the blood from someone Zoe assumed had been with her. Gray, different shades of gray wrinkled or cracked, colored skin. Their eyes varied from a black, lifeless, coal-like to the glassy fogged, gray color. A child that she thought she saw had fangs, moved up to the line that separated them from the lot and pointed at her excitedly. Bending down an adult whispered something into the child's ear and pointed at the woman who had just minutes ago been trying to wash away someone's remains from her hair. Then motioning toward a man holding some kind of beast, they pointed at the woman and the man nodded his head yes. Kneeling down, he pointed toward the woman so that the beast could see the one he wanted, stood back up and released the chain from the beast's neck and said something that Zoe couldn't make out. Slamming to the ground as the beast flew passed her, feeling started to come back in Zoe's left leg.

Cries from the woman pierced Zoe's ears as the woman was hauled to the end of the lot, clawing at the ground. Zoe grabbed hold of the woman's bloody hand, trying desperately to pull her back until with a thud, everything went dark.

Chapter 20

Lori left explicit instructions as to what would need to be done if Megan was leading her and Walter into a trap. Armed with enough firepower to get her out of trouble, but not enough to draw attention, they left just after noon. About half way there Walter handed her a piece of paper that looked to have been scribbled all over by a child. Just as she was starting to think it was Walter's handiwork she noticed at the bottom of the page in large letters was the name Todd.

"Todd said if you follow the lines you can see the pattern." Walter explained.

"Looks like a bunch of scribbles." Megan commented, walking passed them.

"Did Todd say where it started at?"

Walter pointed a finger at a spot and said. "One starts here and the other over here."

"Good boy Todd!" Lori said more to herself than the others.

"You see something in those scribbles?" Megan asked.

"Our Todd is basically a five-year-old in a grown man's body." Lori explained.

"A very big man." Walter added.

"A five-year-old in a very big man's body." Lori corrected herself. "Todd can see patterns in things that we take for granted. Looks like he has been watching your two groups more than any of us knew. Todd has given us a map of what he saw the patterns doing. If he is correct, and he has been in the past, all we have to do is avoid these two areas and we will not meet either of those groups."

"If they move to another area?" Megan asked.

"Then we will have another problem to deal with." Lori said as she started walking again.

"I haven't seen a lot as young as he is." Megan motioned to Walter, trying to change the subject.

Walter stayed a few feet in front of them rarely looking back. To Walter it was a blessing to get away from the others and he thought it was for Lori too, after seeing what she had turned into. He had been scared for his own wellbeing for the first time since he became whatever he was. He did not think he had reason to be too scared of anything that they would meet ahead.

"He has been like that since we met him a few weeks ago." Lori replied.

"And you, how long have you been…like this?" Megan asked.

"I was bitten a few weeks back by a two-point-zero. Turned my shoulder into this type of skin but that was all, until yesterday." Lori replied.

"So you're like a new born with the type of power and control that I saw?" Megan asked amused. "How can that possibly be? It took me months to be able to do what you did to me outside of the barn this morning."

Walter slowed a little, listening in as best he could. "Don't count on the control part too much."

Lori laughed a little nervously and replied. "Yea, lack of control yesterday was almost a bad thing for Walter."

"So Wally got a bit of a scare then?" Megan asked.

Walter stopped where he was and turned around. "Walter not Wally!"

"Ok, Walter it is." Megan replied with a smile at Lori. "Up here we can turn and go between the houses. I think that will somewhat hide where we came from."

Lori looked over the alley way running behind neat rows of houses. "Looks safe enough, what do you think, Walter?"

Walter turned without answering and made his way to the alley keeping the same pace and distance between him and Lori as before.

******

Virginia watched Lori's group leave from the walkway suspended from the top of the barn. Their progress seemed slow to her but she figured Lori probably wasn't in a big hurry to get into town. If they had thought the plan out better, Virginia was sure that everyone would have agreed that her and the lads would have been the better choice for this type of mission. *Who better could sneak in and out unseen than her?* Too late to worry over that now, it would be better

151

for Virginia to pick a few spots where she could set up an ambush. If Lori did run into trouble and was beating it back to the farm in a hurry, Virginia figured she could slow up or stop whomever was in pursuit.

Scanning from Lori back to the road leading into the farm, Virginia didn't see a lot of places that would offer both cover and a view of the street. The snow was melting, giving away the hidden drainage ditch on both sides. She couldn't tell from there how deep the slushy water in the ditch was. There was a tree about twenty feet ahead of Lori that could work. Lifting its leafless branches to the sky like a demon, Virginia thought it could hide her from view. The lads, however, couldn't get up there and if someone could see them, then they would find her. No matter how Virginia looked at it, there was no place for her to lie in wait.

"Looks like we're going to have to play it by ear." Virginia said to Zeus who cocked his head to the left as he looked up at her. "Come on boys let's head downstairs and get a few things."

Todd was waiting at the bottom of the stairs, going through an old lunchbox that Doc or Charlie had found and given him back in Rivers Crossing. Virginia went passed him, not wanting to get caught up in conversation. In the RV she found both her and Lori's quills and slung them over her shoulder. A quick check of the crossbow to make sure it was in working order then she was off to the barn door.

"Where are you heading to, looking like your off to hunt bear?" Jermaine asked

"No where." Virginia replied as she tried to walk passed him.

"No where with enough arrows to stop an army?" Jermaine asked, pushing for the truth.

Virginia stopped and gave him her best 'really' look that she could come up with. "It was good for the lads to get out and move around this morning, especially Zeus. I thought I would take them out again."

"Taking the dogs for a walk then?"

"Exactly, I am taking the dogs for a walk." Virginia replied.

"A walk that would call for not one but two quills?" Jermaine asked.

"I thought it would help me if I had a little extra weight. All of that sitting in the truck and RV isn't good for your muscles you know." Virginia replied.

Jermaine looked down his nose at her then at the dogs and returning his glare to Virginia. "You wouldn't be telling me that you're going to follow Lori but that you think I am stupid enough to buy the walking the dog story, are you?"

"Jermaine...you and I have a special relationship. I see you like the older brother that I lost." Virginia replied, trying to look hurt. "No, I am going into the fields on the other side of the farm house. I just thought if I came across a rabbit or something it might be good to have a fresh meal before we leave tonight."

Jermaine knew she was feeding him a line just like he knew there would be very few ways to keep her in the barn. It would be easier to let Charlie deal with this than to stand there trying to trip Virginia up and catch her in a lie. "Ok, just stay on that side of the barn, please. The last thing we want right now is to have that whole town see you and the dogs."

Virginia nodded in agreement and walked out of the door, heading toward the old house. It would add a little time to her plan, but if she could make Jermaine feel better about losing the discussion then so be it.

Chapter 21

The Man in Black stood on the sidewalk in front of the diner he claimed as his own, with his small group of disciples. He was horrified at what he was seeing, how barbaric they had become in a short period of time. This was not the plan that they discussed back in Mississippi. This town was to have only a few of the 'new people' to keep an eye on the resettled human population while the 'new people' would settle in Rivers Crossing. There was no resettling the humans there if they were eating the lot of them as fast as they found and brought them there.

Walking up the middle of the street, leading a bloody human by a rope tied around their neck like a recently bought prized head of cattle to be taken home for the slaughter was against everything the elders had talked about.

"Do you think we should get one before they run out?" Liza asked him as she placed her hand on his shoulder.

Looking over his shoulder at her he could see that the change was finally taking place in her. Even the gray, hard, cracked skin couldn't hide the natural beauty she once had. "The plan is not to eat them." He replied.

"It might not be the plan that you made, but it is definitely what is happening."

Seeing two of the elders coming down the sidewalk he shrugged her hand off and made his way to them. "This was not the plan you guys decided on."

"Tillford, settle down before you give yourself a coronary." One replied. "Plans are like road maps they aren't cut in stone."

"We had a plan to create a new world for us." Tillford said shaking his head in disbelief.

"And we will, Tillford. Let them have their celebration. You go have some fun too, you have done a good job rounding so many up. Before you know it, the word will spread and others like us will come." The other added.

"This makes us no better than what life was before. What happened to the yearly tax idea?" Tillford asked.

"Some of us like the taste of human better than we do cow. Now go down there and see Harvey. I told him to pick a succulent, tender human out for you and your group. Kind of our way of saying good job and thank you."

The Man in Black shook his head no and walked back to his group. He never liked the name Tillford and he was especially not proud of it today seeing what he had helped create. There was no love lost between him and humanity that was for sure. His whole life had been one of growing up on the wrong side of the tracks, never having enough of anything that they needed until he got a job from old Mr. Bufford selling used trucks out on highway eighty-one. Even then, he never felt like people in town treated him like anything other than poor, white trash from across the tracks. Then the apocalypse came and he met more like him. Smart people, who had a plan for a new world where there was no wrong side of the tracks. He was struck by the startling realization that the only thing that had really changed was the tracks had been moved.

Liza came up to him in an effort to offer comfort. The whole group had heard the exchange and knew that it was all different now. "Maybe you and I could go to Rivers Crossing and grab a house. Start over?" Liza asked.

"After we get a fresh human for dinner?" he asked sarcastically.

"If you want cow that's fine with me." Liza answered.

Looking over his group of what he called his "Disciples," he could see why the plan would have never worked. The one called Bubby was definitely not a 'new person' at all. He had the same skin and smell that Megan had. Maybe they were something in between the Mutes and the 'new people.' Either way, he wasn't sure he wanted to deal with Bubby anymore. In truth, he couldn't remember the last time he had heard Bubby speak to him or anyone else. It was probably too late to worry about what Bubby would become. Tillford believed that whatever it was had already happened and that Bubby just followed out of habit anymore.

"Maybe just this once we could go down and look at the fresh humans and think about getting one." The Man in Black said.

Liza jumped up and down squealing like a little kid at the thought. "Can I pick one out?" she asked excited.

"I think the elders have picked one out for us. I am not saying that we will get one." He replied.

Liza grabbed his hand and began leading him down the street toward the old car lot, knocking a few others off their stride as she pulled him behind her.

*****

Stopping just short of the corner house where they could still see part of the old car lot, Megan pointed ahead of them. "There it is, the lot I was telling you about."

Lori stepped a few steps up and tried to take everything in. The first thing she noticed was the Rivers Crossing school busses back out of the way in the field behind the lot. "I need to get a closer look at the lot." Lori said as she moved further down the street.

"I don't think that would be safe." Megan replied.

"I may have friends in that lot. I need to know if they are there or not."

"If they are there how do you suppose we are going to get them out?" Megan asked growing impatient with Lori.

"I will figure that one out when we get up there and if I see one of them." Lori replied.

Leaving Megan standing there alone, Lori and Walter made their way to Main Street and then crossed over to the lot. It took some doing, but Lori forced herself all the way up to the edge of the lot. People were smashed against each other with little room to move. It was hard making out faces unless they had happened to look directly at her. She was trying to think quickly for a way to get them all to rush in one direction, passed her but she couldn't come up with anything that wouldn't end in a blood bath.

Walter tugged on her shirt and pointed toward a black lady fighting her way to the edge. "It's Zoe," he whispered just loud enough for her to hear.

Lori noticed that people were pointing at people in the lot and they would be hauled out by the animal like creatures. *She could do that to get Zoe but would she survive the creature?* Lori wondered. Seeing Megan come up next to her, Lori pointed at Zoe. "I want to save her. She is my friend."

Megan pointed at a man that looked to be the size of a small mountain. "I think he is the one you would tell. They might think something is up if you're picking such an old, scrawny human though."

Lori thought about it for a few seconds. "If I say it is all we need to feed Walter and I?"

Megan nodded her head yes. "That could do it."

Lori and Megan maneuvered up next to the man and Lori tapped him on the shoulder. When he looked down at her she said, "I want that one, there." She pointed at Zoe until he understood which one.

"That one is old, what meat she has will be tough." He replied and pointed out another one.

"No, that's the one I want. It is all me and my boy will need to have. We don't like wasting food." Lori stated as she felt the anger rising inside.

"Suit yourself." He replied as he reached down for the chain.

"I will go get her." Lori stated.

"In there with the humans? That might not be a good idea, little lady. Some of them may have some fight left in them."

Lori let the change come over her once again looking into his eyes with all the fury she could muster. He stepped back a few steps from her and said. "Might be worse for them if they try. You go right ahead and get your food, lady."

Lori moved forward into the lot, she could feel the tension and smell the fear around her as the crowd pushed to get away from her. Everyone moved but Zoe who stared into the people on the outside of the lot with a blank stare. For a moment Lori thought that she might be too far gone to be saved. Zoe wasn't a young woman and had been through a lot before this happened to her. Moving up next to her, Lori placed her had on Zoe's cheek and a tear slid down her face. A wrinkled hand worn from years of age rose up and gently came to rest on Lori's. Eyes lost in despair and hopelessness focused on the face standing in front of her and a light seemed to go off from recognition. "Child run, get away from this unholy place of death." Zoe uttered in a hushed tone.

Lori fought to control the rage rising up inside. *How dare they do this to anyone let alone my friend*, she thought to herself as she bent forward to scoop Zoe up. Lifting her, Lori turned to leave and the man with the creature moved to block her way. "Are you sure that you aren't just trying to save this old woman?" He asked.

"What do you care what I do with my food?" Lori replied. "Stand aside immediately or you will be sorry!"

Moving back, he replied. "It is your funeral lady. Good luck getting through that mob. Not all of them will get a human for tonight." Megan saw the standoff and moved in quick and slammed into him causing the man to stager enough for Lori to go around him. Walter joined Megan leading the way through the pack, trying to open just enough room for Lori and Zoe to fit through. No one moved to stop them, most being more worried about moving to the front and getting their own human. They let her pass without an issue or helped move people out of her way so that Lori could pass by.

Chapter 22

Virginia moved around the house as fast
possible, not letting anything slow her down. With Zeus
keeping pace alongside of her, she cut around to the
back and hugged the barn wall. Once on the other side
of the barn, remembering a gully in the center of the
field, She broke into a full run until reaching it. She slid
down into the icy water at the bottom, followed by a
splash as Zeus and Perseus joined her. For the most part
there was ice that they could stay on. She edged her
way to the top and peeked first back at the barn. Once
satisfied that there was no movement, she scooted up a
little higher to see over the far side where she could
view the town. No movement was good for the
moment. It wasn't an ideal place to lie in wait but it
would have to do for a little while. From the barn the
gully had looked more or less like a crater to Virginia,
now inside of it she could see that it would lead over
near the tree alongside of the road. She loved when a
plan presented itself when none had been apparent.
After resting her leg for a while she would travel down
the gully until she reached the ditch by the tree. The
lads would have plenty of cover between the ditch and
the gully while she scampered up the tree to keep look
out for Lori. The wind was chilling her face and making
her squint so she slid down a little bit. She trusted in
Zeus's ears and nose to let her know if danger was
drawing too near. Lori and she had come a long way
since that first day that they had met Old Bob just down
the street from their house. She wondered if they would
have made it this far without his patient teaching and
understanding. Lori seemed to always have a harder

time learning or following his directions, but Virginia saw him as a father figure and, if she was being honest with herself, it was fun. That was the problem with Lori, She thought, Lori was always seeing life as such a tragedy while she saw a world for the taking. Kill zombies and then move on to the next group of zombies. Kill that group and find supplies before moving on to the next group of smelly dead beings. It wasn't hard to do and she never had to over think it like the others did. Bob understood this, why else would he have set up all of those little strongholds along the way? He had to have a place to rest up for the next group he ran into. Even Virginia knew there was no way to fight twenty-four hours a day, every day.

Zeus and Perseus perked their ears up and pointed their noses toward the heavens, bringing Virginia's attention back to the moment. She closed her eyes, trying to zero in on whatever it was that they could hear. A slight melodic whistle of a tune flowed pass them up above. The whistle struck a decrescendo and played away on the wings of the wind. Virginia sat upright and grabbed her crossbow sitting in the snow next to her. The harder she strained to hear the notes playing the more she knew it wasn't music. They were screams being carried out of town with the breeze.

"Come on boys, time to move." Virginia said as she moved down the gully toward the tree. She stayed as low as possible so that her head didn't pop up over the edge in places where the gully ran shallow. She moved as quickly and stealthily as she could, careful not to lose her footing in the slushy mess beneath her feet. Zeus stayed as high as he could, he never liked getting his paws wet; while Perseus charged up the middle letting the water splash all around them.

When she reached the ditch Virginia slid down to a seat while she worked to catch her breath. Zeus, panting heavily, sat down next to her and put his paw in her lap. "Ok boy, we can take a rest for a little while." She said as she patted his head. Deciding that there would be plenty of time to rest once she was up the tree, Virginia raised her head up just over the side and searched for any movement in town. Not seeing any signs of life or movement, she climbed the tree, hauling her quills and crossbow up on her back. Finding a fork in the branches that offered both a comfortable seat and a great view, she sat with one leg straddling the branch. Looking around trying to judge how much cover the perch offered, Virginia decided that it was as good as anyplace she could see looking up at the higher branches.

*****

"Can you see her?" Jermaine asked as he came up the last few steps to the walk way.

Charlie pointed over at the tree. "She is up about halfway in the tree."

"Well, I guess you called that one right." Jermaine joked.

"I think we both knew she was going to go no matter what anyone said."

"Yea, I just never would have thought that Virginia saw me as the easy one out of the two of us." Jermaine said. "Is that where we can get to the roof?"

Charlie followed Jermaine's finger down the walkway to the hatch above the walkway. "Yes, I don't think we would need to go all the way out. Should get a fairly decent line of sight just poking your head and the rifle up."

Jermaine held the box of shells up and said. "Let's hope so, Boo only had about a dozen shells left."

"Let's hope for our sake that we don't even need to use that thing. There will be hell to pay with Lori if anything happens." Charlie replied.

"Our sake?" Jermaine asked. "This was your crazy idea to let her think she was pulling the wool over our eyes buddy."

"You didn't take much effort to convince." Charlie said as he broke into laughter. "You were a rock of resolve, let me tell you."

"Ok, I may have cracked pretty easy under the pressure. You made a good point about us watching and knowing where she was instead of her sneaking off and us not knowing." Jermaine sat down on the walkway, feeling the vibrations travel down to the far end. Looking up at the thin steel cords connecting to a small square plate, he prayed that they would hold fast.

Chapter 23

Moving passed the last person who could have raised an objection to Zoe being carried away, Lori found the smorgasbord of scents and sights were having an effect on her body. She could smell death knocking on the door to collect her old friend's soul. From behind her the breeze was bringing a tantalizing whiff that every taste bud in her mouth began watering for. The inner turmoil from yesterday with Walter returned with a vengeance, calling out and then screaming inside Lori's head for fresh meat. The hunger echoed around, bouncing off her skull in time with every beat of her heart. Lori looked around for a safe place to lay Zoe down. A place where no one would bother the old woman while she took just a few minutes, maybe fifteen at most, to satisfy the urges trying to beat her into submission. Seeing a large evergreen tree planted a little too close to a house and judging that to be as good a spot as any, Lori started to make her way over to it. Just as she made it across the street onto the parkway a hand touched her from the left. Having been so caught up in the euphoria of the possible kill, Lori had been blindsided by the creature now touching her arm. Fangs showing, grey bloodshot eyes blazing with rage locked onto the hapless creature. In the blink of an eye Lori had planned and was now starting to execute the final maneuver the creature would ever see.

"Bubby, is that you? What are you doing here?" Megan asked as she forced her body between Lori and Bubby. The smell of fear was so strong that it was throwing gasoline on the fires of rage inside of Lori.

Megan turned to come face to face with what she thought was her own personal view of hell on Earth. "Lori, this is Bubby. He is a friend, Lori, and can help us get out of here." Megan hoped to get through to a part of Lori that was still willing to listen.

"Bubby, what are you doing over there?" a girl said from the back of the crowd and started for them.

"Liza, don't come over here, please." Megan called out to her. The girl just kept coming without a care in the world.

"Oh, it's you, Megan. If you're planning on coming back, you should know that I will be getting a place with Tillford."

Megan was surprised at the slow rate Liza's brain picked up on things. She knew that she shouldn't be after how much time they had spent together but she was. "Look Liza, this isn't the best place for you to be right now. I am just catching up with Bubby and then I am going." Megan replied.

"Your friend didn't pick a very good human did she?" Liza asked looking down at Zoe.

"We don't need anything more." Megan replied growing irritated.

"Tillford could get you a healthy one if you would like me to ask him. It would be no problem at all." Liza stated

"No, this one is fine and who in the hell is Tillford?" Megan asked

"Oh that's right, you don't know him by that name do you?" Liza asked. "We hardly even noticed that you left this morning did we, Bubby? Tillford would be who you know as the Man in Black."

"No wonder he never told anyone his name." Megan replied. "No, please just let us be on our way."

Liza opened her mouth to reply as Lori's hand gripped her by the throat cutting off her air flow. While Megan had pleaded with her, Lori's brain worked out the ways to silence this annoying thing for good. Bubby moved in and bit Lori's arm causing just a brief loosening of the grip and Liza was free, screaming at the top of her lungs.

Megan drew herself in close to Lori's ear. "If we don't run they will kill your friend."

From the cobweb filled dusty, depths of a place long since forgotten in Lori's brain she heard that. The love and respect that she had come to feel in the short time that she had known Zoe thrust the human side back on top in a turbulent, partial control. "Head for the barn as fast as you can." Lori said to Megan and Walter. "You can come or stay, doesn't make a difference to me." Bubby looked from Lori to Megan not understanding what she had meant.

"Run Bubby, we have to get out of here." Megan yelled as she took off.

Lori could hear the cries of terror followed by outrage. Looking over her shoulder she could see that Walter, Megan, and the creature called Bubby, were keeping pace if not threatening to overtake her. After a few left turns through snow covered yards and right

168

turns back onto the street, they were headed to the barn. A shot rang out, kicking up snow next to Lori but she kept running as hard as she could. If they could only make it down by the barn Charlie and Jermaine might be able to slow the advancing mob closing in.

Just passed the last of the town streets, Lori felt her legs give way as her feet lost traction in the slush. Zoe's breath was shallow and slow but she had a good grip on Lori's neck. When it became obvious to Lori that there was no way to stop herself from falling, she tried to arch her back, twisting so that she would bear the impact of the fall instead of Zoe. With a thud, and a wince from Zoe, they plowed into the slush covered corner. Lori tried to sit up but found it to be too slippery so she began working her way onto her side when a male voice said. "Let me take her so that you can get up." Lori stared into the gray fogged eyes of a large man wearing a long black coat like something out of an old western movie. Handing Zoe to him, she rolled over onto her hands and knees, climbing back to her feet just as Megan and Walter caught up. "What way?" the voice asked. Megan pointed down the street out of the town.

******

Rubbing her hands together as fast as she could Virginia then clapped them together with a *smack*, trying to drive the numbness away. The crack of a gunshot startled her, threatening the fragile balance that kept her in the tree. Seeing Lori running down the street towards her, Virginia raised the crossbow, loaded an arrow and sighted first on Lori then moved back behind to the creatures advancing. Taking a deep breath and the slowly exhaling she drew a bead on the nose of the creature. Another deep breath and another slow exhale, she began to squeeze the trigger, then pulled up as Megan reached back grabbing the creature in an effort to speed it up. Shaking her head, Virginia raised the crossbow back up and started over from Lori on back. Fifty yards or so further up the street the mob was now visible following the dog like creatures they had run into by the river. Sighting on the lead one, she knew that it would have to be a clean shot to the eye if it was going to drop it. It was out of range so she waited patiently for it to come into a distance she thought she could land the shot. Glancing down at the Lads she wondered if maybe for them she should retreat back to the barn. Having never experienced any sort of doubt from one of her decisions, Virginia felt like someone had kicked her in the stomach. The options were to hold fast and do what she could to help Lori or to start back to the safety of the barn in an attempt to save the dogs. There was a slim chance of her making it out alive if she stayed in the tree until the last minute but Virginia had no confusion on Zeus' chance of out running the creatures all the way back to the barn. Perseus would have a better chance but Zeus had slowed down a step or two of late.

Shaking the doubts from her head, Virginia sighted the lead creature again. It was a little far for her she knew, and could hear Old Bob scolding her. *"Deep breath, Virginia, nice and easy now."* She calmed her mind and found her sweet spot, lining up the shot . Her lungs expanded to capacity and then calmly exhaled as her numb finger squeezed the trigger and let the arrow fly. In that moment she could see the arrow fly as if all time had slowed down to a crawl. Whizzing over Lori's group, just above their heads, and dropping to the correct height to meet the target the arrow made its mark. It struck the creature just above the eye, then ricocheted up and over. Old Bob would have been right again, she thought, slinging the quills and crossbow over her shoulder so that they would not be in the way for the climb down.

*****

Mesmerized by the way the sun reflected off of the field of white snow, Charlie found himself lost in thoughts of the past—A past where there were no walking or running corpses trying to eat or infect him; a time when nothing made him happier than to hear his sweet Annie's voice first thing in the morning or to lie in bed watching her sleep before he got up. Through the corner of his eye he noticed movement from the tree that Virginia was in. Zeroing in with the binoculars he could see her come down fast and call out to the dogs. Moving down the street further, Lori and a small group were running as hard as they could followed by creatures and a mob. "We got big trouble, Jermaine!" Charlie shouted at him while nudging the sleeping man with his foot.

Stretching his arms above his head Jermaine asked. "What's happening?"

"I think the whole town is following Lori back to the barn and they don't seem happy." Charlie replied. "Take Boo's rifle and put down anything that gets too close to them. I will try to meet them with the truck and bring them back." Charlie yelled over his shoulder running down the stairs talking two steps at a time.

Jermaine climbed up into the hatch leading out on the roof and laid the rifle out in front of him. Holding his hand up to block the sun, he knew this was a bad thing going down. Raising the rifle to his shoulder and looking through the scope he could see Virginia and the dogs coming back at full speed. Perseus was leading the way while Zeus stayed close to Virginia. Back behind them was Lori and her group, followed a little too close for his liking by a creature. The mob was closing in after that so he decided to take care of the closest threat first. He slid the bolt back and inserted the cartridge, then slid it back in place with a click. Jermaine took a good look before firing the first shot that hit the creature in the head, causing it to explode in a brief shower of red. Jermaine watched as Megan slowed down to reach for the creature. The pack caught up and enveloped her. It seemed as though she struggled for a moment but there were just too many. She didn't stand a chance. A mass of writhing monsters concentrated on the point where he had last seen her. He didn't care to think on what was going on. He closed his eyes for a moment, biting his lower lip, then opened his eyes again and tucked his cheek down onto the rifle's rest, just behind the sight. Moving back, he selected the next target, slid the bolt back ejecting the spent shell and replaced it. *Boom*, another creature hit the ground in a shower of red and white as it smashed down, sliding in the snow. Jermaine repeated the process until there was just one shell left. Holding it for the next target that grew closer than the others he hoped that Charlie would make it to them in time.

Chapter 24

The truck careened in a wild slide from the left to the right as Charlie gunned, turning onto the road. Behind him the snow kicked up like the wake behind a speed boat. From this level the mob looked like it had thousands and was advancing a lot faster than he had thought. Coming up to Virginia and the dogs first, Charlie slowed down and yelled. "Get in now, we have to get Lori too!"

"Go get her and pick me up on the way back." Virginia replied running past the truck.

Charlie shook his head in disbelief and mashed down the gas pedal, sending slush raining down on Virginia and the lads. Judging the distance between Lori and the truck Charlie started to slow up a little, not enough to make him get there too late but just enough so that he could swing the truck into a semi donut and face the other way. Just before he reached them he pressed the brakes all the way down and swung the steering wheel hard to the right. The truck swung in a fast arc and almost went into the ditch. Stopping just before the pavement under the snow became gravel, he Jumped out and waved furiously for Lori and the others to get into the truck. Lori jumped into the back followed by the man carrying Zoe and then Walter.

Plums of wet snow shot up until the tires dug through the snow, reaching pavement and catching traction. They lurched ahead, sending everyone in the bed crashing to the side. The distance between the mob grew until Lori felt the truck slow down and Virginia and the dogs came into view. Not wanting to deal with

Lori at that moment, Virginia jumped into the cab with Zeus and Perseus.

"Just for future reference, I watched you from the barn through the gully to the tree." Charlie said matter-of-factly.

Virginia smiled back at him not knowing what to say or if it would matter. She was sure that there would be plenty of words said with Lori if they got out of this. Pointing up ahead at the RV coming down the farm road toward the street Virginia asked. "What is Jermaine doing?"

"If he is thinking what I have been thinking, he is going to lead the way out of this place." Charlie replied.

"Wouldn't we be better off inside of the barn?" Virginia asked.

Charlie shrugged his shoulder and replied. "Not sure how long we could hold out against a group that large. If they were just zombies, maybe."

Lori knocked on the back window of the truck and waited for Virginia to slide both sides of it open. "Anyone have a spare gun I could borrow?" Lori asked then looked over at Virginia. "You and I have a lot to talk about later when we stop."

Charlie laughed and pulled his pistol from the side pocket of his coat, handing it back through the window. "Let's just worry about getting away for now."

174

Taking the gun from Charlie, Lori made sure that Zoe was pressed up against the back of the cab where the wind would be blocked. The man that had helped them had taken his coat off and draped it over Zoe like a blanket. He still had some kind of sweat shirt on that zipped in front as far as Lori could tell. Moving back by the tail gate Lori tried to steady herself as best as she could. The man tapped her on the shoulder and motioned for her to move back off of the tailgate. Once Lori had moved he reached down and pulled the tail gate closed with a bang that made Walter and Zoe jump.

Pulling two pistols out from under the sweat shirt he positioned himself by the tail gate. "Now we can use the tail gate to steady ourselves. I have twelve bullets and I am pretty sure you don't have more than sixteen so every shot matters."

Lori draped herself over the tailgate and took aim. After she fired her first shot and was aiming the second she introduced herself. "My name is Lori, by the way."

"Pleased to meet you, Lori. You can call me Tillford or most people back home just called me Tilly."

"You know this isn't going to make much of a difference." Lori remarked as she fired another round.

"No, not much at all. Maybe a few less to catch up to us though." Tillford replied.

*****

175

Jermaine had fired a shot and couldn't help but be pleased with himself. Somehow he had actually taken down two creatures with a single shot. *No one will ever believe me when I tell this story,* he thought as he reached for another shell. His heart sank feeling an empty box and instinctively he looked down on the walkway below him to verify that he hadn't dropped any. Seeing nothing but an empty walkway, his mind raced to remember if any of the other rifles had a scope. Convinced that only Boo had one like that, he looked for anyway that he could continue to help. That was when it dawned on him. This mob wasn't just the run of the mill zombies or two-point-zeros. They were like Lori, so that meant that they could think and act just like any other person. The barn would become less of a place to make a stand and more of a tomb for all of them trapped inside. The RV was still loaded with supplies from yesterday's attempt to leave for the next stop on the map. All he had to do was pull the RV out, close and lock the barn doors behind him, and hope that Charlie caught on to what he was doing. As long as no one showed up driving something that could catch up to them, everything would work out fine.

Running down into the bunker Jermaine found Tressa sitting at the table talking to Todd as he drew pictures on the back of an old paper sack he had found in the barn.

"Tressa, can you gather all of Todd's stuff and meet me in the RV as quick as possible?" Jermaine asked.

Tressa looked up surprised and asked. "Is there trouble?"

"Trouble doesn't even begin to cover it." Jermaine replied, "A stranger came down the street and told us a little more about the people in the town."

"The ones I saw last night I bet you. I bet you anything that's what it was," Todd said excitedly.

"Yes, the people that you saw last night, Todd." Jermaine replied. "Lori went into town with Walter and that girl to have a look around and check things out."

"Todd, get your stuff and let's go, follow Jermaine to the RV." Tressa said, without waiting for Jermaine to finish. "You can finish once we are all safe." Tressa added, pulling a few things that she had brought in the night before together and pushing Todd to move faster. They followed Jermaine up to the RV and climbed in. Todd thought he should sit in the front seat riding shotgun because he was a boy, but changed his mind with a stern look from Tressa.

Pulling the RV out of the barn, Jermaine was nagged by the thought that he had forgotten something. It wasn't anything of his that needed to be loaded, he didn't own very much since the apocalypse and he wasn't one to collect new things. What was the point when he was constantly on the move? There was something that he had seen inside the barn on one of the mornings where he had awakened hours before anyone else; something that, more than likely, he had seen and thought nothing about it because it didn't mean very much to him at the time. Now for some reason it was at the back of his brain trying to make its way to the front and it was driving him crazy. *A button in a glass case, there was a red button in a glass case.* Jermaine thought to himself trying to remember where he had

177

seen it. *Back by the generator, I saw it back by the generator.* Jermaine froze in his tracks wondering why the button was such a big issue in his in his thoughts. *It was probably a master off switch for the generator,* he thought, but couldn't shake the bothering question of why he would remember it that of all moments.

Looking to see how much time he had before Charlie would be at the end of the long driveway, he decided that if he could run back there and just take a look he would still have time to meet Charlie, if only just at the end of the driveway. Throwing the door open he ran back into the barn straight to the generator. It took a few minutes for him to find the locked glass case hidden off toward the back of the machine. Just under the case was a small handwritten sign that read: *In extreme emergency press and evacuate immediately.* Jermaine took a step back and remembered that he had to meet Charlie before he turned down the driveway leading back to the barn. "I think even Old Bob would see this as an extreme emergency." He said to himself as he picked up a hammer laying on the bench beside the generator and smashed the glass case. Pushing the button, he had half expected some kind of voice to start announcing a warning with a count down. *Hell it probably doesn't do anything at all,* he thought running back to the RV.

Turning onto the street, Jermaine tried to keep a close eye on where Charlie was. Once he was sure that Charlie had caught on, he turned his attention to finding the street. He had seen another state route that bypassed Clarksville a little way off to the east of where they had been. He thought they could follow that for fifty or so miles and then cut back to the west, picking up several cross roads that would put them back on course to the next stop on Bob's map.

Feeling confident that Charlie would follow without the mob catching up, Jermaine stared ahead into the solid white field before him looking, hoping for, a sign or something that would let him know the street he sought was there.

Chapter 25

Charlie watched the tail lights on the RV glow and slide hard to the right, followed by the backup lights coming on. Jermaine was backing up, turning right; it didn't look to Charlie like it was a street but he would trust Jermaine that it was. After all, if it wasn't he would know soon enough. There was no way the RV would make it through deep snow off road.

"Where is Jermaine taking us?" Virginia asked.

Charlie shrugged his shoulders. "Doesn't really matter where right now as long as it is away from here." In the rearview mirror he could see the mob was no longer following them, they must have taken interest in the barn. A few creatures seemed to not give up the hunt but were falling farther and farther behind. Charlie flashed his bright lights several times, trying to get Jermaine's attention. On the fourth series of flashes the brake lights lit up on the RV as Jermaine brought it to a stop. Charlie pulled the truck up just short of tapping the rear bumper. He hopped out and told Lori to get everyone inside of the RV as he scanned the area around them for danger. "You can ride with me and save yourself some trouble until a later time or go face the music." Charlie said to Virginia.

"I am going to stay in the truck but want to put the lads in the RV. It has been a long day for Zeus." Virginia replied.

Coming out of the RV, Jermaine almost walked right into the man carrying Zoe. From the looks of him he figured the guy was almost the same size as he was, maybe just shy of it but pretty close. He began reaching for his gun but Lori walked up. "Jermaine, meet Tilly, he is going to be traveling with us for a while."

Not sure how he felt about that. Jermaine just nodded his head and let the guy pass by. He walked over to where Charlie was standing. "Yesterday we didn't want to sleep in the camper because we had to many people and thought it would be crowded."

"Today we have two more people inside the same camper. Don't complain to me, I was following your lead today." Charlie replied with a smile.

"Do you want to lead the way or follow?" Jermaine asked.

"Been following this far, you might as well keep leading." Charlie replied.

Jermaine started back to the RV when the sky turned a brilliant reddish-orange back toward the farm and the Earth shook with a thunderous boom.

"What the hell!?" Charlie said.

"That Old Bob had the place booby trapped. I thought it might help even the odds a little bit in our favor. Wasn't expecting it to be that big." Jermaine said with a chuckle. "What's with the guy carrying Zoe?"

"Came back with Lori, I haven't had a chance to ask about it." Charlie replied.

"No, I don't guess you have. I will find out what I can."

Chapter 26

With her feet on the dashboard and her head leaning against the cold glass, Lori tried to stretch out and get some rest. More had happened in the last two days than she could honestly remember happening since she and Virginia had left their home with Bob. If it was all a dream Lori knew that it would be a nonstop nightmare that she'd never wake up from. And Virginia, Lori didn't even want to think about that right now. Sometimes she thought that Virginia's antics were growing worse with each new day. Yes, it had been a good thought to lie in wait to save the day if it was needed. In truth all she had really accomplished was placing her life and the dogs in jeopardy. Lori let out a long sigh and told herself to just let sleep overcome her for now. When that didn't work she opened her eyes and stared at the passing fields until that proved to be too monotonous.

"Where are we heading?" Lori asked Jermaine.

Handing Lori the maps, he replied, "I am not one hundred percent certain, to be honest."

They both looked at each other and began laughing. "Your plan was to just drive?" Lori asked.

"Well, I did look at the map for a minute or so first. Looks like this road will cross a few that we can take to get back on course to the next stop." Jermaine replied.

"It will cross all of the main roads." Tillford said, standing between the seats just behind them. "I have traveled these roads a lot in the last six months looking for small towns."

"What about this spot here?" Lori asked pointing out a forest preserve. "Looks like there is a lake there too."

Tillford thought for a few minutes. "Pretty good sized parking lot. Plenty of cover from the trees on two sides with the lake on the third. You could see someone coming from the road in enough time to prepare to meet them."

"How far off do you think?" Jermaine asked.

Scrunching his face as if he had just sucked a lemon, Tillford replied. "At this speed, few hours at most."

"So just before dark then." Jermaine added. "No signs of anything to worry about?"

"I camped by the lake a few nights, great largemouth bass in it. Couldn't seem to pull myself away. Of course, that was a few months ago." Tillford replied.

"Then I think we should stop there for the night and plan for tomorrow." Lori replied as she climbed out of the passenger seat and stepped around Tillford. Tressa and Todd had been in the back with Walter and Zoe. Lori wasn't sure that no news from back there was good or bad. Having put it off as long as she could, it was time to face the music.

"How is she doing?" Lori asked.

"Feels like she is burning up and hasn't said anything yet." Tressa replied holding a damp rag to Zoe's forehead. "We could really use Doc, or someone with a little medical background."

"I know." Lori replied. "We will have to do the best we can for her."

*****

Virginia thought for sure that she saw something moving through the fields, low to the ground, fast, and moving with purpose. Closing her eyes for a few seconds and reopening them, the movement would be gone.

"Are you doing ok with all of this?" Charlie asked Virginia.

"Why wouldn't I be ok with it?" Virginia replied.

"Wasn't too sure that you would be." Charlie said.

Feeling tightness in her chest and no small amount of sadness Virginia raised one tremoring hand up toward the sky. "I promise you that if it needs to be, I will put Lori and Walter down without thinking about it."

"It sure doesn't seem like we will need anything that extreme."

"We don't know that yet. There is no way possible that you could know that for sure." Virginia said.

"I think we both know your sister well enough to be certain that if there was a chance that she could harm any of us, she would leave first."

With sad eyes that pitied Charlie for letting his feelings cloud his judgement Virginia looked at him. "For now I will wait and watch. If you're right, then this isn't even an issue."

"I understand what you are saying Virginia. I just want to make sure that we give it time to see how it works out."

She shook her head yes and looked at Charlie again. From the very first day she had liked Charlie and Boo more than she thought was possible. Boo was like Old Bob, so that was an easy one for Virginia to understand. Charlie wasn't like anyone she had ever met before. He couldn't shoot very well, had no idea of how to survive in the world that they lived in, and he trusted everyone and everything around him to be what it advertised. Nothing like her, Bob or Boo in any way shape or form. Yet there was something about Charlie that made her want to believe too, Made her want to see the goodness left in the world around her. If someone had given a choice to Virginia of who she wanted to be standing with in the end, Charlie would be on the list. Not very high up on the list, she smiled as she thought, but on the list nonetheless. "As long as the lads are ok and don't react then I will hold off."

"That is all I am asking for." Charlie replied.

"Charlie, you're in love with my sister and you think this will end with you two having a family." Virginia added at the last second.

Caught off guard, Charlie changed the subject. "What did you think you were going to do up in that tree? What were your plans for the dogs?"

"I guess you could say that I didn't plan that out very well." Virginia replied.

Feeling like he took back the upper hand, Charlie contined. "That is my point in a nutshell. Sometimes you need to think things out more before you react. Jermaine and I knew exactly what you would do and damn near how you would do it. The tree was a surprise but we should have figured on that."

"You didn't stop me." Virginia replied.

"I think we both have learned that stopping you is almost impossible. So we looked out for you in the best way we could." Charlie said.

"You do know that I rode with you so that I could get out of a lecture, right?" Virginia asked.

Smiling like he had been caught sneaking a brownie off his mother's kitchen table, Charlie replied. "You got me there and we both know you have one coming that there will be no getting out of."

"I know, so I am going to try to get some rest until we stop. Lori can go on for hours when she wants to, repeating the same thing over and over." Virginia leaned her head against the window, trying to fall asleep.

Chapter 27

Tillford pointed over to the left of the highway, making sure that Jermaine saw the forest preserve coming up. The park was gilded in gold as the sun reflected off of the thin layer of ice that formed on top of the melting snow.

"Looks beautiful, let's hope it is safe." Jermaine said.

"Let's hope." Tillford replied. "I can go take a look around if it will make you feel better?"

"Once we get settled down I can go with you." Jermaine replied.

Tillford thought about it and was going to say that he really could travel faster and smell if there was danger by himself. He decided instead that it was a good sign that this guy wanted to go along.

"What about over there?" Jermaine asked, pointing to a spot near the lake and a park pavilion. "I think we could light a decent fire in the middle of that, kind of stretch our legs a bit."

Tillford looked back over his shoulder to see if he could still see the entrance and the highway. "I think that would work for me, almost hidden from the entrance but just enough of a view for us."

Slowing the RV down, Jermaine yelled to the back "We are here everyone, your home for the evening."

Lori started to let Zoe's hand go when she felt the slightest bit of a squeeze. Looking down into Zoe's empty, sad eyes, Lori said, "We are going to rest here Zoe, you're safe now."

"No one is safe anyplace, child." Zoe replied. "They came into the school acting like they just needed a place to stay for the night to get out of the storm."

"We got you away from them, Zoe. Please believe me that for now we are all safe." Lori replied.

Zoe struggled to raise herself up then lay still for a second before putting everything she had into rising. Knowing that she would not stop until she was up, Lori placed her hand under Zoe's back and raised her up to a sitting position. "Help me out there to the table, Lori." Zoe commanded in a pleading voice.

"Jermaine, can you come help Zoe to the table?" Lori yelled up front.

Jermaine came back with Tillford and they both very gently took an arm, helping Zoe stand. After thinking about asking Zoe if she thought that was best, Jermaine knew that it would be easier to get Zoe to where she wanted to be. Up the short hall they went, holding Zoe up as she took baby steps on wiry legs. Reaching the table Jermaine reached behind, placing his hand just under her armpits and slid her into the booth. "There, how is that?" Jermaine asked.

"Thanks son, thank you two very much. Let me rest for a few and I will see what kind of meal I can come up with." Zoe replied.

"I was planning on cooking something up as a treat to welcome you back." Jermaine replied.

Zoe smiled and made a "pfffft" sound as she looked toward Tressa. "Maybe you can make dinner, Tressa?"

"I will, don't you worry about that at all." Tressa replied.

The lads moved to the door and everyone knew what that meant. In that magical way they knew that Virginia was coming up to the door. With a creak, the RV door opened and Charlie came in followed by Virginia.

"Before you start, there is plenty of time for us to talk about today." Virginia began before Lori could say anything.

Lori walked over throwing her arms around her pulling her in so close that Virginia wasn't sure if she would be able to breathe. "I am not even saying anything about that." Lori said as she turned and gave Jermaine a big hug. "Thank you and Charlie for knowing how her brain works. That was some good shooting."

"I was all for stopping her until Charlie pointed out that we would have to either hog tie her or lock her in a cabinet. Hard to do either one with those two dogs around." Jermaine replied as Lori broke off the hug.

"Going to be tight in here tonight." Lori stated as she sat down across from Zoe.

"We were talking about that earlier." Charlie said looking over at Jermaine.

"I can stay outside." Tillford offered.

Jermaine pointed towards the pavilion. "If we can get close to that, someone can stay on watch with a fire going under it."

"Road curves around pretty close I think." Tillford replied. "We can take a look to make sure."

"Why don't we do that?" Charlie said, moving around the dogs to the door when he felt a large hand grab him by the shoulder.

"Tillford and I will take a look, why don't you stay here." Jermaine said.

Once outside Tillford went over to a metal park garbage can and knocked the lid off. He proceeded to dump the trash out on the snow. "If we can find some wood to burn this will keep us warm while we are out here."

"Just happen to have some wood on the top of the RV." Jermaine replied. "Not much, but enough to help get it going."

Tillford rolled the can under the pavilion and kicked away the snow so that the can was sitting on the pavement. Jermaine climbed up the ladder on the back of the RV, then threw down several pieces of wood.

Carrying as much as he could in one load, he threw the logs into the barrel. "Now for the best part," he said as he pulled out a small brick like package wrapped in plastic. He peeled the plastic off then pulled out a lighter from his pocket to light it. Getting the edged caught aflame he dropped it into the barrel with the wood. In an instant the fire started picking up in size and heat with a flash. "Never leave home without them." Jermaine said with a smile.

"If we run short there is always that." Tillford said, pointing at the picnic tables around the park. "Now I know and you know there was a reason why you wanted to be out here with me. I don't think you see me as a big threat anymore."

"I am just curious as to what was going on back there in Clarksville is all. These folks in there have become like family to me and I look out for my own." he replied.

"Fair enough, what do you want to know specifically?" Tillford asked.

"What the hell is going on with you, Lori and the kid?" Jermaine asked.

Tillford shrugged his shoulders. "I think we are mutations of the original virus. Human and zombie I guess you could say."

"Like the two-point-zeros?" Jermaine asked.

Tillford shrugged again as he dug out a smoke, holding it up for a light. "Not sure what that is."

"They are like smarter, faster zombies." Jermaine replied.

"Oh, we call them mutes because they are a mutation from the original infected."

"If they are mutations, what are you then?"

"I guess I am a further mutation. Or perhaps the human immune system in me fought back harder, holding onto more human traits. I really don't know." Tillford replied.

Holding his hands over the fire, feeling the warmth surge up through them, Jermaine inquired further. "How do the changes happen? You know, where your normal one minute and a...."

"Creature?" Tillford finished for Jermaine. "I don't know how it works or how to explain it."

"So what were you all doing back in Clarksville?"

"It was supposed to be a new town in a new era. A town made up of mostly humans with people like me keeping an eye on them." Tillford replied. "The rest of us and any more like us that we found, were going to settle into Rivers Crossing."

"You think there are that many of you out there?" Jermaine asked.

"More than you would ever imagine."

Jermaine motioned for a smoke, taking it, he placed it between his lips and cupped his hands to block the wind as he lit it. He took a deep drag, held it in for a second, then slowly exhaled. "The girl that came down the street early this morning talked about some kind of market." Jermaine stated looking at Tillford for an explanation.

"I can't explain that so I won't even try. All I can really say is that wasn't supposed to happen, ever." Tilford replied.

"But it did happen." Jermaine pushed.

"I know it did, that is why I helped Lori and the old woman get away. I didn't and don't ever want part of what was happening there." Tillford added.

"That's good enough for me, but you will have to convince the others of that." Jermaine replied.

Chapter 28

The morning sun covered the land in glittering sparkles as it illuminated the inside of the RV. An uneventful night was a welcomed change from the previous day's events, especially for Lori. She had felt completely exhausted after they ate the hodge-podge of freeze dried meals that Tressa had packed back at the barn. After another meal of freeze dried eggs they were on their way once again.

The drone of the RV motor was rarely broken up by voices. Occasionally Todd said something to himself as he played with two cars he had found back in Rivers Crossing. Lori, who was driving, finally broke the silence. "Zoe, do you see a town or anything coming up?"

Zoe, who had insisted on riding shotgun when they left the forest preserve, reached into the glove compartment for the map. With arthritic hands still stiff from being held out in the cold, she unfolded the map in front of her. Then she folded it so that only the area that they were in was visible. "Looks like if you take a right on Route Ten we run into a small town. Doesn't even have a name on the map as far as I can see."

"Let's hope that it has a gas station or something. We are down to a quarter of a tank." Lori replied.

"No gas in the other truck?" Zoe asked.

"The gas was in the back of Boo's truck. With everything going on, it kind of slipped our minds, I guess." Lori replied.

Zoe pointed ahead of them at a sign. "There is the sign for it now."

Lori slowed the RV down so that she could safely make the turn without sliding off the road. She glanced into the mirror, making sure that Jermaine had seen her and had followed.

"It doesn't look very far from here on the map." Zoe said.

Lori nodded her head that she understood, as she eased her speed back up. The RV shook as it drove over the bumpy road causing her to ease back off a little.

"This road must be in bad shape under the snow?" Zoe asked.

"Not sure what it is like under there," Lori replied, pointing at the ice covered street. "It has been trampled down then froze like that."

"There it is!" Zoe stated, pointing at the town ahead. "Not much to it."

The front end of the RV lurched and a front tire felt like it fell in a hole as a crash came from the kitchenette area. A cabinet jerked open, spilling out boxes of freeze dried meals onto the sink. Charlie and Tressa came forward from the back, looking over Lori and Zoe's shoulders. "What the hell do you think did this to the road?" Charlie asked.

"It doesn't matter right now. I am going to have to stop for gas up there." Lori replied, pointing up at the only gas station on the street. Lori made her way into the gas station coming to a stop by one of the pumps. She knew if there was no power then they would have to go scavenging around.

Zoe turned in her seat so that she could look at the three of them and asked. "Would it be ok for an old lady and Todd to stretch our legs while we are here?" Lori started to answer that she didn't think so, when Charlie answered. "I don't think that would be a problem at all. Can you two stay near the RV, just in case we need to move quick?"

"I think we can follow instructions, how about you, Todd?" Zoe asked.

Todd jumped up almost stepping on the dogs and knocking Virginia off her seat. "I will do whatever Miss Zoe tells me to do. I promise, whatever she says." Todd replied.

"I will check the area around us out with the dogs." Virginia pulled her coat on and grabbed the crossbow.

"Well, it's settled then, let's go have a look see." Zoe stated.

Virginia opened the door, letting Zeus and Perseus out first, then followed. The station lot was trampled, just like the road coming into town. Zeus took the lead as he sniffed the air around him for signs of danger. It was harder for him to pick the zombies out because Lori and Walter were too similar. They were different enough that he knew who they were, but similar enough to mask some of the scents he was looking for. Moving away from the RV with Perseus hanging tight next to Virginia, he was picking up the creatures by the river mixed with the zombies. They had been everywhere and left traces all over the place. Virginia grew impatient and walked passed Zeus, causing him to nearly nip at her. Thinking better of it, he took the lead again. Something didn't seem right to Zeus about the building Virginia was heading to, and it wasn't like her to keep walking past him. Finally having enough, he did nip at her pants, holding firm until she stopped. "What has gotten into you, buddy?" Virginia asked as she pulled her pants from his mouth. "Go ahead and lead if that's what you want."

Approaching the glass door, Zeus stared in, trying to see any movement. He sniffed the air wildly for any signs that he was missing when the glass vibrated with a loud slam against it.

"That's not a good sign at all." Jermaine said coming up behind Virginia.

"Especially since I think we need to get in there to turn the power on." Charlie added.

"Pumps dead?" Jermaine asked.

"Doesn't look like there is power anyplace." Charlie replied walking up to the door. "Someone locked them in there or they locked themselves in and then turned."

"How do you want to play this then? Shoot the glass out and go in?" Jermaine asked.

"I can go in first" Tillford offered. "They should think that I am one of them, or at least that has been how it has worked so far."

Charlie thought about it for a few seconds as he looked around. "If there are more they will come when the shot goes off."

"Then we should get everyone back in the RV that doesn't need to be out of it." Jermaine said motioned back toward Todd and Zoe. "The rest can take up positions watching the station and our backs."

"Tressa, can you help Todd and Zoe get back into the RV for a few minutes?" Charlie asked.

Not knowing why, Tressa started to get them back inside. Just as she closed the door and turned around the shot pierced the morning silence and the glass exploded into the station, dropping the zombie that had been standing by the door. Within seconds, four more came from the back where they could not be seen from outside. Virginia dropped one with an arrow to the eye while Charlie, Tillford, and Jermaine took care of the rest. "If the first shot didn't call them the next three should do the trick." Virginia observed as she and Zeus walked passed the three men.

The air inside of the station was stale and putrid like the inside of a meat locker that had broken and was left to sit for months. It was small and built before stations had turned into mini marts. Two or three shelves where snacks and motor oil had once been lined up neatly on display were now empty. Charlie went to the back room where he thought the zombies had come from and found the fuse box on the wall behind an old metal desk. Finding all the fuses on, he returned to the others. "Not the fuses," he said as he knelt down to where an old gas can sat on the bottom shelf. "Looks like we are scavenging."

Chapter 29

They split up into three groups, Charlie and Tillford, Lori and Jermaine and Virginia and the lads with Tressa. Todd and Zoe were safely locked inside of the RV with instructions to lay on the horn at the first signs of trouble.

Walking away from the station toward the way that they had entered town, Zeus and Perseus were leading the way. Zeus hung back near Virginia while the old Perseus seemed to be returning as he ran off in front then turned bolting back to them. Virginia thought even Zeus was glad to see Perseus acting like Perseus. He didn't nip him like normal when Perseus got close.

"How do we do this?" Tressa asked, walking next to Virginia.

"Let the dogs lead and we follow them. Zeus won't let us walk into trouble without letting us know first." Virginia replied.

"What do we do if we find gas? We don't have a gas can." Tressa said.

"I was going to look for gas cans in the houses. You know, like they would use for the lawn mowers." Virginia replied.

"Go into the houses?" Tressa asked. coming to a halt in the middle of the street.

Virginia laughed. "You don't have to come in, you can wait outside while the dogs and I look around."

Tressa's mouth dropped open in shock. "You're going to leave me outside by myself?"

"You will be ok, believe me. You have your gun and we will come the minute you fire a shot." Virginia replied.

"Ok, I will trust you on this one. I haven't ever gone in looking for trouble like you guys have." Tressa said as Virginia patted her on the shoulder.

"Good, stay right here and we will be right back." Virginia said as she walked up to a garage door. Bending over she tried to raise the door. Standing back up and looking back at Tressa she said. "Must have a garage door opener, we will have to get in from the inside." Tressa squeezed her pistol so hard that the color was leaving her fingers as she watched Virginia open the front door, following the dogs inside. She turned in a slow circle so that she could see in every direction. The sun felt good on her face as she noticed the calm, eerie silence around them. Even the absence of birds in the calm blue sky was unsettling. It had her on edge enough that she nearly pulled the trigger on her pistol when the door shot open with a rumble.

"Found one and it is full!" Virginia yelled, coming out of the garage carrying a large old gas can.

"We can go back now?" Tressa asked excitedly.

Virginia started to tell her that they should probably see if they could find one more. Then thought taking Tressa back would be a better option. Virginia knew that she could move faster if she wasn't keeping an eye out for her.

"We can go back and put it into the RV. That will let us check on Zoe and Todd." Virginia replied.

*****

Coming up to an old Chevy Dually, Tillford reached into his coat and pulled out a slim jim, smiling at Charlie. "I like to come prepared for anything." Sliding it down between the door and the window, he started moving it around. Charlie went to the other side, pulled out a crowbar and shattered the passenger window. Brushing the glass off the seat, then sliding over, Charlie unlocked the door and replied. "Me too."

"Well, if that is how you want to do it. I like to show a little finesse." Tillford said.

"Sorry, my door was actually unlocked. I just wanted to see your reaction." Charlie replied. "I found the crowbar sitting behind the seat."

Reaching up Tillford lowered the sun visor and a key fell into his lap. "I don't even want to know if my door was unlocked."

"See if it will start, we can probably drive it back and just syphon the gas from the tanks directly into the RV." Charlie said.

Tillford put the key in and turned it as the motor roared to life. Smiling, he closed his door and headed back to the gas station. "You notice how trampled all of the snow is everyplace here?" Tillford asked.

"Yea, I don't really know what to make of it. Just looking to get on the move as fast as we can." Charlie replied.

"Usually the dead ones like back at the stations stay pretty calm around me." Tillford continued.

"They didn't seem very calm when they charged the door." Charlie stated.

"I know, that has me worried. Whatever this is, it keeps mutating. You can see it all around us. Maybe that kind has mutated again?" Tillford asked.

Charlie shrugged his shoulders as they pulled into the station next to the RV. Seeing Tressa and Virginia, he motioned them over. "I think we have enough gas in both of the tanks on this to get moving again once we have syphoned it."

Virginia nodded ok as she turned back toward the station with Tressa in tow.

"You think it is safe enough to let Todd come back out?" Tressa asked Virginia looking around the area.

"I think so, we will just keep him by Zeus and Perseus, he will like that." Virginia replied.

*****

Lori and Jermaine came up on a large house with a porch that ran all the way around to the back. In the driveway sat a newer model truck and three cars. Lori went to the first one and tried the handles, finding it locked. On to the next, she found that too, was locked. Jermaine waved his hand at her. "I am going to check the garage for a gas can."

"You're going the wrong way then. The garage is over there, behind the house." Lori replied.

"First I am going to check the house for canned goods or box mixes. I don't think I can handle one more freeze dried meal." He replied.

Lori laughed and went to the next car.

Jermaine tried to look through the large oval window in the front door for any shapes that were moving. The beveled glass made it impossible for him to tell with any amount of certainty so he turned the knob and pushed the door forward. The heavy door swung open with hardly any effort at all, coming to rest against a stopper on the wall. Raising his gun up in front of him, Jermaine entered the foyer, looking to the right into the living room and then quickly to the left, into what looked to him like a home office or den. Satisfied that nothing was in either room he advanced into the foyer until he came to the dining room. It was also empty and Jermaine guessed that the door on the other side of the large ornate dining table was the way into the kitchen. Trying to walk as softly as possible on the wood floors, he passed around the table. With each step the sound of his boots on the wood echoed through the room until he was one step away from looking into the kitchen. Sliding his feet over until he stood square in the door the urge to vomit rose from deep within his bowels and Jermaine lost it. A dark red with bits of white flesh coated the entire room. On the floor next to an island were the remains of something no longer identifiable. Backing from the door he felt his stomach tie into a knot again as the second heave worked its way up and out of him. Breathing deep in a last ditch effort to regain control of his body, Jermaine closed his eyes for a second then forced them open and advanced into the room. Each step brought a squish of the remains under his feet that grew louder as he walked. Moving to the pantry, Jermaine kicked the flesh out from in front of the door as he felt another heave start to come. Once open, he could see that the pantry was empty. Turning to decide which cabinet looked more promising, he decided that maybe the one next to the range would hold something. Like the pantry, it was empty, so he threw the process out of picking one and just started opening all of the doors. The sooner he could get the hell out of this room and house, the better. Opening the fridge, Jermaine was forced back by the smell. How, he wondered, could it possibly smell worse than this room? There was nothing in there that could be eaten so he opened the freezer. Again, a smell hit him smack in the face, causing his eyes to water. Only this time he was rewarded for braving the stench. He smiled as he found a full bottle of vodka in there for the taking. Pulling it out and opening it, he took a swig to settle his nerves. It burned his throat going down but hit the spot. Leaning back against the counter, he raised it to take one more swig before returning to Lori. Outside the kitchen window for as far as he could see was the largest herd that Jermaine had ever seen. He included the one at Rivers Crossing in that assessment. They were just standing there, not moving one way or the next. It was like someone had turned them off or put them in standby mode. *He had to get to Lori before she made any type of noise that would awaken the herd or alert them, he thought.*

He put the cap back on the bottle and shoved it into a coat pocket as he made his way back through the dining room. Sliding on the wood floor as he rounded the table, he only just stayed on his feet thanks to the high backed chairs he caught himself on. Entering the foyer, he didn't check to see if anything had changed, he just kept heading toward the front door with only one thought, to get to Lori and for them to get away clean and unharmed. As he passed a mirror that had gone unnoticed the first time through, Jermaine caught a reflection out of the corner of his eye coming toward him. Turning just in time, he blocked the creature with his forearm. Blood washed down to his elbow as the creature sank its teeth deep into his flesh. Lifting the barrel of the gun up to the creature's temple, it took everything to not pull the trigger. Lifting it higher up he brought the butt of the grip crashing down on the skull over and over as chunks of skull and flesh sprayed all over and the creature fell to the floor with a heavy thud. Feeling the wound where a gaping hole replaced a significant portion of his arm, Jermaine shook his head in disbelief at his stupidity. Knowing that he should have gone out the same way he came in wasn't helping matters. Putting the gun back into his coat pocket Jermaine stumbled out of the front door, falling down the stairs.

"Jermaine!" Lori yelled when she saw him hit the ground, taking off running to help.

Getting back up just as Lori reached him, Jermaine looked at her. "We have to go now."

"What happened to you?" Lori asked.

"I got careless and walked into something that bit me." Jermaine replied.

Lori stopped and looked into his eyes as a tear rolled down her cheek. "I am so sorry Jermaine."

"Don't count me out just yet. I think I thought of a way to stop it from spreading. Either way we have to move fast and get back to the others."

"We will move as fast as we can. I don't want you to get your heart pumping fast, causing it to move through your system quicker." Lori replied.

"Lori, on the other side of that house I saw the largest herd that I have ever seen." Jermaine said.

Chapter 30

Pulling the hose out of two tanks and coiling it up, Charlie thought they had all they needed for now. "That's about as much as we're going to get. Should be enough to get us to the next town."

Tillford nodded his head in agreement. "Where do you think the other two are at?"

"That's a good question, I wish they would get back so we can get back on the road." Charlie replied.

"Should I honk the horn until they come?" Todd asked excited at the thought.

"Nah Todd, let's give them a little longer before we start doing that." Charlie replied.

"There is more than enough gas left in the Dually to go take a ride and find them." Tillford pointed out.

"Sounds like a plan." Charlie replied, handing Tillford the keys. "Virginia, can you get everyone else ready to go?"

"Sure." Virginia replied. "Looks like they are ready."

Tillford drove down the street in the general direction that they thought Lori and Jermaine had gone. At the cross street, taking a left then following that as far as they could until it dead ended into a field.

"Which way now?" Tillford asked.

Charlie didn't answer right away, sitting there as still as a statue. "You hear that?"

Tillford held his breath so that he wouldn't miss the slightest noise then exhaled and replied. "Sounds like someone crying for help or the wind playing tricks on us."

"What direction do you think it's coming from?" Charlie asked.

He closed his eyes and took a deep breath that he held for a moment while his listened intently. "I would say from that way." He pointed out Charlie's window.

"That's my guess too. Could be one of ours in trouble." Charlie replied.

Tillford started the engine and turned the truck toward where the noise was coming from. Moving slow to not have their presence be known, they cruised up the road.

"There!" Charlie said. "Do you see it over by that can?"

Bringing the truck to a stop, Tillford squinted and strained his eyes to see what Charlie was pointing at. It looked like the figure started waving an arm in the air. "I see it, let's go." Tillford replied.

Before Charlie could say anything Tillford was out of the truck, running at full speed. Before Charlie was even out of his seat, Tillford was yelling for him to pull the truck up. Tillford ran straight for the figure crying out, paying little heed to his surroundings.

The hairs on the back of Charlie's neck began to stand up once he was out of the truck. He couldn't help but feel like death was standing behind him. His mind began to imagine that it could hear the scythe cutting through the air to reap his soul. Peering over his shoulder, Charlie saw the first one come out of the shadows. It was joined by another and then another until he could no longer keep track for sure. Screams of agony snapped the icy death grip of fear that held Charlie in place. Raising his gun, he squeezed off a round at the closest, then squeezed off another. Screams became more desperate, almost mind numbing. Charlie lost all sight of Tillford. Chaos reigned supreme all around; inside Charlie was as calm as a lake on a windless day. Targets presented themselves just long enough for Charlie to squeeze off a round, dropping them. Shots echoed off to his left so Charlie shifted his feet and took aim. Seeing Lori and Jermaine standing there, he let his hand fall to his side. Lori went over to where Tillford had been and poked around a little. Coming back, she said. "We need to get back to the station."

"Tillford?" Charlie asked.

"Not much left to him." Lori replied, starting the truck and backing up until she slid into a turn on the street.

"The one that was crying for help?" Charlie asked.

"He was probably dead when you guys got here." Lori forced the Dually into drive and fish tailing down the street.

210

"We found the herd that has trampled all the snow around here. Let me tell you it is huge!" Jermaine stated.

"You couldn't tell they were here?" Charlie asked Lori.

"No, I didn't have any idea or scent of them. I don't think Tillford did either or that back there would have ended differently." Lori replied, sliding the Dually onto main street and into the station lot. "Charlie, you drive the truck, I will send Virginia and Perseus to ride with you."

As soon as Perseus came out followed by Virginia, they were on their way. Charlie took the lead thinking that he would be able to cut a path through the herd if it closed in around them. Just outside of town they found the leading edge. They were just standing alongside the road, watching as Charlie and the others approached. Keeping the truck as far toward the opposite side as he could, Charlie kept a close eye for movement. There was no breaking toward them, no surge onto the road, just the heads all turning in unison as they passed by.

"Ever see anything like that, Virginia?" Charlie asked in a hushed tone close to a whisper.

"Never." Virginia replied. "What happened back there?"

"Tillford and I heard some kind of cries. We followed the sound and come up on a man or something laying in the street waving an arm at us for help." Charlie replied.

"When you went they sprang on you, right?" Virginia asked.

Turning his head in shock, Charlie looked at her. "How did you know that?"

"This guy named Jack that was with us in the beginning with Bob told us about something just like that. He said the two-point-zeros had set a trap for them. You go to help the crying man and they come at you from all directions." Virginia replied.

"That was how it happened all right." Charlie said more to himself than to Virginia.

"When did Lori and Jermaine get there to help?" Virginia asked.

"The end I think, not really too sure now." Charlie replied.

"Then you did ok for yourself, Charlie!" Virginia play punched Charlie in the arm.

"Thank you, I think…" Charlie replied, trying to force the images out of his head.

"You're alive Charlie and that's all that matters. You stood your ground against a group of two-point-zeros, that is something!" Virginia continued.

"Have you ever, you know, been by yourself against them?" Charlie asked.

"I used to go out with the lads and hunt them. Well, I did until Bob and Lori found out about it. They weren't all that happy with me." Virginia replied.

"You hunted them on purpose?" Charlie asked not wanting to believe what he was hearing.

"It is a lot easier than you would think once you know how they move." Virginia replied.

"And you know this?" Charlie asked staring at her for a second.

"Trust me Charlie, you could do it too. They always set a half dead person or one of their own as the bait to draw you in. Once you reach a certain point the close the trap on you." Virginia explained.

Charlie shook his head in disbelief. "Come at you from all directions?"

"Exactly!" Virginia replied. "The secret is to set yourself up outside of the trap and drop the bait. Works best when they use one of their own but will still work if it is a wounded person."

"Then what?" Charlie asked wanting to know more.

"They come out from hiding when the bait is dead and they know you're not coming. Drop them as soon as they show themselves and let Zeus and Perseus deal with the ones you miss." Virginia continued. "It really is that simple and easy."

"Wow! Jermaine was right about you." Charlie stated.

"Oh yea, and what was it he said about me?" Virginia asked.

Charlie smiled. "You were not the girl to mess with and it is great to have to you in a fight."

"I think I will take that as a compliment. So thank you both for thinking that." Virginia replied.

Chapter 31

Zoe sat on one side of the table with Jermaine facing her from the other side. His arm was laying out before them on a folded up blanket. She jabbed at the wound in different places with stiff fingers that barely closed. Jermaine winced on a few of pokes but managed to hold it in on most. Turning her hand over she placed the back against his skin, just outside of the bite, to feel the heat. She gingerly stood and placed her hand against his forehead for a few seconds. Sitting back down, Zoe looked across at Jermaine and the sadness returned to her from when her great nephew had been bitten. "Do you want us to get Virginia to ride with us?" Zoe asked.

"Nah Zoe, it isn't going down like that." Jermaine replied.

Todd came forward and wrapped Jermaine in a bear hug that smothered him. With tears flowing freely, Todd held as tight as he could.

"Don't you worry Todd. It's going to be alright. I have a plan to beat this bite before it beats me." Jermaine said as Lori helped pull the crying Todd off of him.

"Son, there is no way to beat this." Zoe stated. "I can feel the heat traveling up your arm while we're sitting here." Poking the skin just below Jermaine's elbow then poking an inch lower with more force she sat back. "Cool and then blazing hot."

Pointing to the spot that Zoe had just said was still cool. "So it hasn't moved to this part yet?"

"Not as far as I can tell with these old hands and fingers. I am not a doctor, Jermaine." Zoe replied.

"Closest thing we have to one now." He replied smiling. "So, let's say we cut the arm off at the elbow, what happens then?"

"You lose your arm, son. What are you asking me?" Zoe pleaded.

"Zoe, I am asking you if I would be alive and missing one arm or will I be dead missing one arm?"

Zoe could see the desperation in Jermaine's eyes, Like Albert a short time ago, he was really asking the old woman to say that everything was going to be ok. "There is no guarantee that you won't still turn." Zoe forced out finally.

When Jermaine was little and found himself filled with fear from a nasty thunderstorm he would run and hide in the back of his closet. He wanted to be in the back of that closet now waiting for the deep voice of his father to tell him that the storm was passing, that he could come out from hiding. "I got nothing to lose by doing it then."

"It will be painful because we don't have anything to cut it with." Zoe replied.

"There is a circular saw in the tool box in the back of Charlie's truck. We can use the power from the RV." Jermaine replied. "We need to do this soon before it moves too far."

Zoe looked up at Lori for an objection. Finding none she looked back into Jermaine's eyes. "Tressa honey, if you see any place that looks safe enough to stop could you let us know?"

"I saw a sign for a feed warehouse a little way back." Tressa replied. "Do you think we have gone far enough to be stopping?"

"Well, Jermaine, will a feed warehouse do?" Zoe asked.

"Tressa, I think we will be good now, please pull into the warehouse when you see it." Jermaine replied ignoring Zoe's question.

The RV shifted to the right hard, feeling like it had left the ground as the back end swung around toward the front. "Hold on, it kind of just came up on me." Tressa yelled back as everything came to a stop. Within seconds Charlie and Virginia were pounding on the door to get in.

"What the hell happened back there?" Charlie asked bursting into the RV.

"We are all good." Jermaine replied. "Have to do a minor surgery so we thought we could stop for the night here."

Looking at the gaping hole where Jermaine's forearm had once been, Charlie felt the wind knocked out of him. "Jesus Jermaine, I didn't know that you were bitten. Why didn't you say something back there?"

"You know me, Charlie. I don't want anyone worrying for nothing." Jermaine replied.

Zoe stood up and shushed Charlie with her hand. "Where are you wanting to do this at? In here or out in the snow?"

Jermaine looked around and shook his head no. "Let's do it in the snow, I don't think anyone wants to ride around sitting in my blood."

"Do what out in the snow? What are you two planning to do?" Charlie asked, confused.

"Virginia, could you go look in that large box in the back of Charlie's truck for a saw?" Zoe asked.

"Circular saw, woman! I can't do this with just any old saw." Jermaine stated.

"You're going to cut his arm off?" Charlie asked. "Have you guys lost it?"

"If I don't cut it off, Charlie, I will turn. If I do cut it off there is a chance that I will live and not turn." Jermaine replied growing teary eyed.

"Look at Lori, she didn't turn!" Charlie stated.

"Charles, that is even slimmer odds of happening. By the time we find out for sure it will be too late for him." Zoe stated.

Charlie tried to wrap his head around what was happening. It took him back to the arguments that he had with Doc about Annie. "Then let's at least see what is in the building and do it in there. That way we are all in an enclosed place, safe from the elements and any surprises in the night."

"Fine Charlie, I can go along with that. You and Virginia go check it out and come back and let us know." Jermaine replied.

Virginia came back in with a dirty looking, worn out circular saw that the name had long been worn off.

"Come on Virginia, let's take the dogs and check out the building." Charlie said.

*****

A brick façade covered the front of the building with a large overhead door on the right side. Window slits rose from the ground up to eaves on either side of a glass door on the left. Looking through the windows revealed nothing, the light entering from the headlights cast a faint glow illuminating a single desk. Charlie put his hands on either side of his face, pressing against the glass hoping that any movement would stick out. He leapt back raising his pistol when Virginia shook the door hard, trying to force it open. "Sorry." She whispered.

Charlie rolled his eyes at her.

"We could just bust it open?"

"You take the dogs and go around that way. I will meet you in back on the other side." Charlie said. "Be careful Virginia."

Virginia took the lads and went around the corner and then stopped. "Perseus, go with Charlie." The dog looked back at her, then Zeus, and then he was off around the front to catch up with Charlie.

Zeus's pace was brisk because he wasn't picking up anything in the air that told him danger was near. The side of the building was an unbroken line of corrugated metal that Virginia thought went on for miles. Out of the shadows a figure on four legs came towards them at full speed. Zeus wagged his tail and set off after it. Perseus had decided that he would save everyone the trouble and went past Charlie around the building until he found Virginia again.

"I guess the way is clear, boy?" Virginia asked Perseus as he tried to get Zeus to play with him.

"There is a metal door back here that isn't locked." Charlie said from the corner.

"Are we going in?" Virginia asked.

"We can follow the dogs in and see if we can open the overhead up front." Charlie replied.

Chapter 32

The overhead door went up and two silhouettes came out framed by orange and red flickering light. Tressa and Lori raised their guns up until two smaller shapes came running up from behind.

"I found some broken up pallets so I dumped the trash out of the metal cans." Charlie said pleased with himself. "We get light and heat!"

"I will get the others and meet you inside." Lori said.

"No need, we can pull the truck in so that we have more light for the surgery and back the RV in. There is plenty of room for both." Charlie replied. "Keys are in the truck; I will take care of the RV."

No one said a word as Charlie climbed out of the RV and pulled the overhead door closed crashing with a slight bounce when it met the pavement. Pulling a screwdriver from his pocket that he had removed when opening the door, Charlie slid it back into its home securing it from opening. Tressa ran the extension cord from inside the RV out to an old wooden table they had found and placed directly in front of the truck. Jermaine sat there tightening some cargo straps they had found to hold his arm down securely; one across the bicep and the other just below the elbow. Tressa checked them when he was finished and gave the thumbs up. "Are you sure about this?" She asked softly, so just Jermaine could hear her.

"As sure as I will ever be." Jermaine replied. "My other choice is for you to take that pistol out and bury a bullet in my brain."

Tressa bent over and gave him a hug without saying another word. She moved out of the way as Zoe came out of the RV, holding her hands up like a surgeon. "Zoe, we are using an old beat up circular saw. Do you really think your hands being clean with stop me from getting an infection?"

"I tried to clean the blade but it is stuck on there." Zoe replied as she picked up the saw, hands shanking from the weight. Placing his free hand on top of hers, guiding the saw back down onto the table, Jermaine reassured her. "I got this Aunty, you just be ready to step in when its done."

Tears began to flow as she set the saw down and brushed her aging hands across his forehead and nodded ok. Lori stepped up and placed the bottle of vodka down next to Jermaine's free hand. He could hear the cap unscrew as she pulled it off and set it down.

"Thank you, Lori." Jermaine said as he raised the bottle up and took a large gulp then slammed the bottle down on the table. "Let's be done with this then." Picking up the saw, Jermaine squeezed the trigger once and the saw sang out as the blade took off. Smiling once at everyone around the room he motioned his head towards the bottle. "Could someone move that please? I don't want it to get broken or anything. I figure I will need it in a moment." Just as Lori lifted the vodka up the saw sang out again as Jermaine raised it above his elbow and then plunged it down. Blood showered over everything, flying off the blade in an arc as it bit into his flesh, coming to a stop as it hit the bone. Screams echoed through the warehouse as Jermaine became light headed and consciousness slipped away.

Zoe stepped up and managed to press on Jermaine's finger as she lifted the blade up enough to free it from the bone. Leaning forward, placing all of her weight into it, she pressed down. Blood showered over her and into her eyes as she pushed down then lifted, pushed down and lifted again until pieces of wood from the table could be seen in the thick pool of blood. Setting the saw on the ground, Zoe undid the strap from Jermaine's bicep and looked over at Virginia. "Child, did you put that piece of metal into the fire like I asked you?" Virginia nodded her head yes. "Be careful now and get that for me."

Virginia grabbed the blankets that Zoe had given her earlier and wrapped them around the part of the flat metal not in the fire. Pulling it out the fire barrel, the glowing red end smoked as it met the chill of the air. Walking it over to Zoe, Virginia started to hand it off.

"Charlie I need you to help me hold this arm still. Tressa when I say go, you slap that iron onto the stump."

Tressa moved forward and took the bar from Virginia, being careful not to burn herself or the girl. Holding it just inches above the stump she was shaking like it was a stick of dynamite ready to explode.

"Now child, do it now." Zoe commanded and Tressa brought the glowing metal down to meet the bloody stump. Jermaine screamed to consciousness as the sizzle of hot metal met the tissue, filling the air with an over powering smell of burnt flesh. His head raised for a moment while screaming then Jermaine collapsed back onto the table.

Looking over the stump and poking it with her fingers Zoe though the wound looked decently cauterized. "It looks ok as far as I can tell. Let's get him cleaned up and into the RV. He will need to rest now. I will keep an eye on him."

Charlie helped carry Jermaine into the RV and placed him in the back bed. He was surprised when Todd moved in and helped. For an instant he saw Todd as one of the adults until Todd smiled at him the way a small child does when they are pleased with themselves for a job well done.

Zoe sat on the edge of the bed with a damp cloth wiping the sweat off of Jermaine's brow. "I will holler if I need you guys."

Charlie nodded his head OK and followed Todd out into the warehouse. Lori and Tressa had taken blankets and the few sleeping bags that they had and were setting them up in a circle around the barrels. Off away from everyone else a couple of sleeping areas were made up for Lori and Walter. When Charlie objected Lori shut him down before he could present an argument. "Walter and I were covered by Jermaine's blood too. It's not as easy for us to just ignore that like the rest of you. We will be better off over there for tonight. Charlie, please don't argue this." The one thing Charlie had learned about Lori was that she rarely changed her mind once it was made up. This was one of those times so Charlie let it go.

Chapter 33

Tressa found some old shop rags in the closet of the front office and a bucket. Kneeling down on the concrete, she scrubbed the blood and bits of bone and flesh into a small pile. Scooping them up with a dustpan, she emptied it into the fire. After thirty or forty minutes the spot was still visible but not to where it would scare Todd every time he walked by. There were no words to describe how proud she had been when Todd jumped in there to help Charlie move Jermaine into the RV. Every now and then a part of Todd would sneak out to offer tiny glimpses of the man he would be if not for his condition. It was that part of him that carried Virginia and Zeus back to the school with the herd on his heels the entire way. Across the way, sitting too close to the fire, Todd was playing with his cars trying to lure Walter into a game with him, parking one of the cars next to Walter's leg and talking to him like it was his car. Now and then Walter would answer in a made up voice that would send Todd howling with laughter. Walter would smile and shove the car back over to Todd causing the whole process to start over again. Charlie had walked by during the laughing attack and ruffled Todd's hair as he passed.

Tressa would have never thought that there, in the midst of death and ruin all around, that Todd would find his place. If something happened tomorrow, Tressa thought, she could rest in peace knowing that Todd would be taken care of. Tressa climbed to her feet as one of her knees let out a loud pop. Stretching for a few minutes to work out the kinks, she motioned to Todd.

"Todd, we should turn in now. May be a long day tomorrow helping Jermaine."

"Do we got to, Tressa?" Todd asked, pleading for more time. "Wally and I just started playing is all."

Tressa noticed the slight look of irritation on Walter's face but he didn't correct Todd. If anyone else had called him that, including Lori, there would have been a swift rebuke. "Yes, come over here. I made your bed up and brought your pillow out for you. You can play with Walter in the morning if he wants to."

"Can we. Wally, can we play in the morning like Tressa says?" Todd asked.

Walter rolled his eyes a little. "Sure we can, Todd, as long as I get the blue car."

Todd looked at both of his cars for a second, trying to decide if that was agreeable to him then replied. "Doc told me to never let anyone else play with the blue car." Turning it over slowly in his hand, he looked it over. "I guess he would be ok with you playing with it. Do you want to sleep with it?"

"That's ok, Todd. Why don't you hold onto it until the morning." Walter replied as he got up and walked away.

"Ok, see you in the morning, Walter. You can wake me if I am not up, ok?" Todd yelled out as Walter laid down where his bed had been made up.

Lori came out of the RV and sat down next to Charlie. "Virginia and the dogs are going to stay in the RV tonight, in case Jermaine turns." She paused to see what Charlie would say. When he didn't say anything she continued. "I was hoping you could stay in there as well."

"Believe me, I think Virginia could handle anything that came up in there." Charlie replied.

"I believe she could too but Jermaine is a big guy and really strong. Sometimes, when they first turn, they still have all that strength. I am not sure that Virginia and the dogs could handle that much brute force alone."

"If it makes you happy, Lori, I will go stay in the RV tonight." Charlie replied smiling. "Besides I think the vodka is in there."

"Save some of that for Jermaine. I think he is going to need it when he wakes up."

Charlie climbed up into the RV and found the dogs sleeping on the table which had been made into a bed. Virginia was sitting on the floor in the hallway leading back to the rear bed where Zoe still sat next to Jermaine. He was out like a light. Deciding that the best place for him would be the passenger seat up front, Charlie first grabbed the bottle of vodka off of the counter. He plopped down into the seat and swiveled it around so that he had a good view of the entire RV, all the way to the back. Reaching into the glovebox, he pulled the map out and opened it to where he thought they were. Charlie traced his finger to where the next stop on old Bob's map was. If they took turns and drove around the clock they could possibly make it in the next day, depending on the roads getting better the farther south that they went. Leaving the truck here would give

228

them three drivers, possibly four, depending on how Jermaine felt. Charlie was getting tired of driving and never getting anywhere. It was starting to seem to him that their lot in life had become nothing more than to wander around until they were bitten and turned or eaten by the same creatures. The next place that he found to look safe, the type of place that they could live without issues like today happening, Charlie was going to push for them to stay and make it work at all costs. If no one else wanted to stay then so be it, he would do it alone. Taking a gulp from the vodka bottle, Charlie enjoyed how it burned going down and warmed up his stomach.

"Lori said to remind you to save some of that for Jermaine." Virginia said.

"When did she say that?" Charlie asked.

"Just before she went out to ask you to come sleep in here." Virginia replied.

"You two have me all figured out, do you?" Charlie asked starting to laugh.

"She also said don't think she will be easy on you tomorrow if you're hung over." Virginia added. "And we both know that she meant it."

"That we do, Virginia, that we do." Charlie replied putting the cap back on the bottle. "I said I would sleep in here but I didn't mention that I would be taking the occasional walk to do my rounds. Someone has to keep watch while everyone is asleep"

Chapter 34

After an hour of sitting there, staring off into space, Charlie thought it would be a good time to make a round. Leaving the RV as quietly as he could manage and closing the door slowly behind him he stepped out into the warehouse. Turning to the overhead door, he made sure that the screwdriver was still secure. From there he followed the wall until the door to the front office came into view. Cracking his knee on a desk, he sat down in the chair and looked for movement outside of the window. Satisfied that there was nothing out there sneaking around in the dark, he made his way back into the warehouse. Halfway down the first aisle he came to a whole section of what as best he could say was dry dog food. Not much of the light from the fires made it that far down so he wasn't certain. After the forth aisle, he was certain that there was nothing there beyond livestock feed. Once he reached the end near the first fire, he went and sat down. The only sound was the crackling coming from the barrels as the fires began to die down. Moving over by the back door he found more broken down pallets. He picked up a few pieces to add to the barrels. It wouldn't build a raging fire but he thought it would keep them going for a while. Putting a large piece in each barrel, he stopped upon coming to the one that Walter and Lori were sleeping by. Walter was on the other side from where he stood and from where Lori was laying. Carefully placing the wood inside the barrel then stepping back a few feet, Charlie stopped and looked down at Lori.

In this light Lori's skin looked soft and youthful. Her hair was flowing off to one side, leaving her neck exposed. A smooth line ran down the curve of her back, slightly bulging over her behind, then flowing down to her ankles. Often times Charlie had felt the same level of attraction from Lori that he had from His Annie. Deep down he was sure that Lori had felt the same way about him, she had said as much. He had caught her watching him countless times when she didn't think he was paying attention. The way she cooked, his plate always seemed to have just a little more food than everyone else's. When she sat next to him there was always some kind of subtle contact made.

He looked around the room to see if anyone else was awake and watching him. Charlie felt it would be safe enough to lay down by her if he didn't touch and wake her up. *What possible harm would there be in him sleeping on the concrete?*

Not long after Charlie laid down and fell asleep, he could feel a light breath blowing on his cheek. Opening his eyes, he found Lori had rolled over and was now laying close by. She then threw her arm over him and slid in closer. Slowly Charlie worked his arm under Lori so that she was cradled in his arms. Lori pulled herself in closer, molding their bodies together. Sleep came easy to Charlie as he listened to the Lori's heart beat softly in her chest. Feelings that had long been shoved down into the darkest places of his heart after Annie died, screamed to be released. The warmth from being held while holding someone brought Charlie a feeling of wholeness that he had not felt since he lost Annie. A leg sliding over the top of his caused

Charlie's heart to race in anticipation. He felt Lori's hand pull their bodies together tighter.

*****

Lori's nostrils were flooded with the scent of sweet, fresh meat. It was strong enough that she could taste it with each inhale. Her breathing surged to the point of panting as she tried to get more. Before she could react, the other half of her brain pulled Charlie in closer and tighter, throwing a leg over him, locking the prey in place. *Lub dub, lub dub, lub dub,* her heart pounded faster and harder, threatening to burst free from her chest any moment. She fought to regain control, to slow down the changes that were erupting from inside. She was screaming inside her head for Charlie to wake up and run. No way was left for her to control what was about to happen. Feeling her body slide closer, inching its way over the top of Charlie's pelvic bone, she thrashed within herself to stop. She found herself chest to chest, pelvis to pelvis, on top of Charlie. Placing her hands firmly on Charlie's shoulders, she pushed up until she was arching her back. Head raised to the heavens, Lori opened her mouth and roared so loud that it reverberated through the warehouse. Charlie's eyes sprang open to find a creature of Lori sitting on his chest. Saliva slid down her fangs, dripping into his eyes, as her soulless eyes zeroed in on the pulsating veins in his neck. The nails on her hands dug deep into Charlie's shoulders pinning him down.

Within a moment Virginia was there, aiming the cross bow at Lori while Zeus and Perseus took up positions on either side. Zeus' body tensed as he readied to pounce when Virginia fired. Perseus worked his way over to the other side of Lori, waiting to attack. As she arrived on the scene Tressa raised her pistol in trembling hands, and moved next to Virginia, trying to hold the gun trained on Lori's head.

"Stop!" Charlie screamed. "Don't shoot."

Virginia moved around the barrel, kicking Walter as she passed. He was cowering out of Lori's sight. Virginia brought the crossbow up, aiming at Lori's eye. If she had to shoot, she wanted to make sure that Lori didn't suffer

"Please, everyone back off." Charlie asked as calmly as he could.

Lori's brain took stock of where each threat was located. She assessed which would need to be dealt with first and in what order the others would follow. She would kill the one below her with a swipe of her nails across his throat then move onto the one moving dangerously close by the fire.

"Virginia should I shoot?" Tressa asked, trembling more.

Lori lowered her head down to just an inch from Charlie's face and took a long drag of his scent. Moving closer, she licked from his chin up to the eyelid and then let out an even louder roar.

"Hold on everyone, wait just a second before you do something we will all be sorry for." Zoe said from behind Jermaine.

"Lori, we've been through so much together. Now I know you're in there and I know you can hear me." Jermaine said, pleading.

Lori opened her mouth and let her fangs drag across Charlie's cheek leaving two trace lines of blood as she growled at Virginia. Zeus moved into position so that he could block any assault on Virginia and snapped wildly at Lori before he settled back, ready to pounce.

"Virginia, please lower the cross bow and take Zeus back away from there." Charlie asked.

"I told you that if this happened I would put her down." Virginia replied. Lori snapped at Zeus, causing him to back into Virginia who let the arrow fly wild over the top of everyone. Regaining her balance, Virginia loaded another and leveled it back at Lori's head.

Jermaine made his way over to Tressa, placing his hand on the pistol and pushing it down toward the floor. Taking the gun Jermaine said, "Tressa, please take Todd and Zoe into the RV and lock it up tight."

Tressa did as she was told, gathering up Todd and Zoe, they headed into the RV.

"Walter, can you help me here, buddy?" Charlie asked just above a whisper.

Walter had moved further away during the excitement and wasn't too sure about moving closer. In truth, Walter had wanted to go in the RV with Todd. "The gun shots and the thought that Virginia was in trouble brought her out of it last time I think."

Virginia lowered the cross bow for an instant. Removing the arrow, she set it on the floor at her feet. "Zeus, Perseus, go protect Todd." She commanded. Both dogs remained frozen like statues staring at Lori. "Now! Go protect Todd. NOW. Zeus! Perseus!"

Zeus stood up and looked back at her then walked slowly toward the RV waiting for Virginia to change her mind and call him back. Perseus caught up to him and they both sat between the truck and RV where they could still see Virginia.

Scratching her head wondering how she was going to do this, Virginia finally took a step towards Lori. With her fangs showing that she was not to be trifled with, Lori again roared so loud that Charlie thought his ear drums had burst as his head filled with ringing.

Virginia took one step forward and Lori snapped at the air, snarling. Another step brought fiercer snapping meant to scare her. As her foot touched the ground on the third step Virginia felt the breath being knocked out of her as Lori leapt from Charlie onto her. The fangs felt like four needles pressing into her neck as blood trickled from them.

"I am not going to fight you, Lori." Virginia said calmly as the fangs pressed harder. "If you want to rip my throat out, go ahead. Be done with it already!" Virginia screamed. Lori let loose of her neck and roared into the heavens again. Virginia grabbed the arrow laying just off from her hand on the floor, then released it.

"I can't kill you. You are my sister. I love and you know that you can't kill me." Virginia said. "Do you remember that song that Grandpa used to sing to us in the car?" Lori lowered her head and snarled at Virginia moving her mouth closer. "The stupid one about the doggy in the window?" Lori crooked her head to the left and then to the right looking into Virginia's eyes. "I never could remember the word but you used to just sing away with him."

As quick as she had been on top of Virginia, Lori leapt off of her, knocking the barrel over as she shot across the floor. A moment later there was a tremendous boom as Lori ran through the door leading to the office. Virginia grabbed her crossbow and called the lads to her as she started after Lori. Jermaine grabbed her with his arm, nearly falling to the floor from the force as she smacked into him. "Easy now, I think we might be ok for tonight."

"I know that, Lori isn't going to hurt anyone for now. The lads and I are going to watch outside the door to make sure it stays that way." Virginia replied.

"Let her go, Jermaine. She will rest easier and I think everyone else will too." Charlie said.

"Well, if all the excitement is over, I am going back to the RV. I just cut my arm off earlier you know." Jermaine said, looking down at the bandaged stump and wavering slightly in his stance.

"You go ahead, my friend. I think I will go sit with Virginia for a while. Hell of a thing she did for me here tonight." Charlie said.

"Hell of a thing done by one hell of a little lady." Jermaine replied as he turned back, staggering toward the RV.

Charlie found Virginia sitting on a stool with a dog on either side directly across from the office door. Remnants of the door were scattered everyplace as if it exploded from the force of Lori smashing into it. Charlie threw a few sacks of feed off out of his way, making a seat in the bin on top of the remaining bags.

"Look at what she did to the door." Virginia said.

"Had to have it pretty hard, don't you think?" Charlie asked.

"I think if Lori had wanted to, she could have killed us all without even breaking a sweat." Virginia replied.

"What do you think we should do about that?" Charlie asked. Virginia shrugged her shoulders. "Whatever Lori wants us to do." Standing up, she handed Charlie the cross bow. "You keep watch. I am going to get some sleep." As Virginia walked away she stopped and added. "I could have put her down, Charlie. I had the perfect shot."

"I know." Charlie said as she walked away.

Chapter 35

The nightmares had returned overnight, more vivid than ever. They starting with being pinned down in the bunker, fighting for her life. Teeth snapping just inches from Lori's face, a clawed hand scooping out flesh from her shoulder. It ending with the creature feasting on unsuspecting survivors caught in a hellish trap of death. The only thing that changed was the perspective, leading Lori to believe that she was the creature all along.

Lori blinked her eyes several times in an attempt to clear the sleep away. Stretching her arms up, it became obvious that someone was watching her sleep. Sniffing the air eased her worry as she recognized it to be the scent of Zoe.

"It's not polite to stare at someone." Lori stated.

"It's not polite to try and eat someone, either." Zoe replied with a smile."I have been watching you and Walter sleep for over an hour."

Lori wasn't certain what Zoe meant but some of the haze of yesterday hinted to her she had done something terrible. Sitting up, Lori saw Walter curled up in the far corner still fast asleep. The office looked like a tornado had passed through. Filing cabinets were over turned, pictures thrown from the walls, and everything from the desk she was sleeping on had been swept away. Zoe sat in the desk chair rocking back and forth with her arms folded across her chest.

"What are your plans, child?" Zoe asked.

Lori shook her head no and replied. "I don't know, Zoe. I don't know what it is that I should do now."

"You remember anything from last night?" Zoe asked.

"Bits and pieces, not very much beyond that." Lori replied, holding her face in her hands.

Zoe stood up and placed her hand on Lori shoulder and rubbed up and down in a soothing motion. "Do you remember attacking Charlie?"

Dropping her hands to her lap, she looked up at Zoe, stunned at the idea that she would ever harm Charlie. "No, nothing like that at all."

"You love the boy?" Zoe asked.

"I think I love the man, yes." Lori replied.

Zoe sat back down in the chair and laughed. When she finished she said, "Lori, when you get to my age, all of you young'uns are children."

"I don't think that Walter and I can stay." Lori replied, looking for Zoe to convince her that they should stay.

"I would hate to see you go but I think you may be right. How would you know when something like last night was going to happen? How would we know if it was going to happen before one of us were lying underneath you? Looking up at those fangs that seem to come out when needed."

"I remember Virginia last night. I remember thinking that she was going to end all of this nightmare for me." Lori said, staring blankly at the floor in front of Zoe's feet.

"Is that what you want, child? Do you want us to help end this here and now?" Zoe asked.

Ignoring the question Lori continued, "Virginia was going to let me…or the creature kill her. Why did she do that?"

"Your sister knew that you would never knowingly harm her. Virginia saved you and Charlie last night. She is a remarkable young woman, Virginia is." Zoe replied.

Lori thought about the future she could have had with Charlie. Every way she followed the paths of possibility they ended the same way; always with blood, death, and destruction. There was no way clear that would allow them to have a life together or for her not to end in a battle with Virginia and the lads.

"After we met Old Bob when our brother Jay died. A man named Jack Burrows joined us before we made it to the bunker. Jack was a doctor or scientist, I don't remember which, working on a cure for all of this. Jack had gone out in the field, he used to say, so that he could see it in real time." Lori said, "There was a government lab just outside of Chicago that Jack was from. I think I am going to take Walter and see if there is anything left of it."

"I don't think you will find anything there." Zoe replied.

"I agree, but it would give me a starting point. Maybe Walter and I could find something there that would tell us where to try next."

Zoe felt the tears welling up in her eyes as she listened to Lori. Years of life had taught her that liking something and doing what was right didn't always work hand in hand together. Digging deep into her pocket she pulled out a key chain with the number "seven" on it that held a single key. Zoe placed it on the desk next to Lori and pointed out the window to a lone white van that said "Tri-Co feed" on the side, in large blue letters. "I checked it out while you were sleeping, has a full tank of gas in it."

"You have been busy." Lori said smiling.

"Do you want to wake everyone up and tell them good bye?" Zoe asked.

Lori closed her eyes and shook her head no to the question. The last thing that she wanted was to have to face everyone after what had happened last night. Trying to say good bye would only make leaving that much harder and she knew that Charlie would try to keep her here. At least, part of her hoped he would still try. Lori knew that deep down Charlie saw her as he did his dead wife. Annie had turned and Charlie had to kill her or be killed. No one should have to love and kill two women that have been infected in one life time. "No, I think it's best for Walter and I to just leave."

Zoe shoved a piece of paper and a pen onto the desk by Lori and then pointed over to a cluster of small boxes sitting neatly in a corner among the clutter. "Oh, here I thought you might like to take this too." She handed Lori an old flip phone with a car charger attached to it.

"I don't think I will be able to call with there being no cell coverage and all."Lori said, mocking Zoe.

"Don't you get smart with me, child." Zoe said, joking back, "I am not so old that I have lost all of my faculties. This was my Albert's phone, he took a lot of pictures of the group when he could keep it charged and no one was paying him any mind. I thought you would like it so that you had something to remember all of us by."

She hopped down off the desk and threw her arms around Zoe. "Thank you very much. Yes, I would love to have that and will cherish it for as long as I live." Zoe hugged her back as best she could and replied. "Those boxes don't have much in them. I couldn't carry very much without waking someone up to help me. I put mostly some of yours and Walters personal things, a little bit of food and water."

"That's ok, Zoe, we can get supplies as we go." Lori replied.

Lori spent the next fifteen minutes writing three notes. The shortest one was to Charlie and the longest one was to Virginia while the one in between was to everyone. Holding a pen and writing was odd and somewhat foreign feeling after so long but Lori adjusted quickly. There was no shortage of what there was to say to Virginia. Lori had to cut it off after three pages and move on to the next letter. She said good bye to each person, including Zoe, in a personal way. Charlie's letter, there were no words to say what she felt inside or what needed to be said. After three failed attempts, she settled on just a few simple words. "I will love you for as long as I live. – Lori"

*****

Virginia was the first to wake up so she quietly made her way out of the RV. Tapping Charlie on the shoulder she chided him, "You didn't do a very good job keeping watch."

Charlie shrugged his shoulders looking down at the lads. "What about them? They were sleeping too!"

Virginia smiled back at him as she turned to the office doorway. Noticing that the wood had been swept to the side Virginia turned back toward Charlie. "Has she come out?"

"Not that I know of, and if she did, she sure didn't wake us up." Charlie replied.

Entering the office, being careful to step over the filing cabinets, the first person that Virginia saw was Zoe, sitting at the desk. "Where are Lori and Walter?"

Zoe held up a neatly folded letter with Virginia's name written on the outside. Taking the letter, Virginia leaned against the desk and unfolded it. Reading it over twice she dropped it down to her side and looked at Zoe. "Lori was right. It really was the best thing to do."

"Are you ok?" Zoe asked

243

Virginia thought about it for a few moments. "After last night I think I will be. Now I don't have to worry about her killing me or being forced to kill her."

"Charlie?" Zoe asked.

"That I am leaving to you older folks. I think Charlie thought there was a way that they could build some kind of family together." Virginia replied.

"I think you're right." Zoe replied.

Chapter 36

It had taken over an hour to convince Charlie that he should stay with the group rather than go off alone chasing Lori. Even then, no one could be certain that he wouldn't leave in the night until Jermaine had reminded him of his plan. They would take turns driving the RV only stopping when they needed to fill the tanks up. Once on the road, when they could clearly see that the tire tracks left by Lori had turned off heading in the direction of Chicago, did Charlie mention following her again. As soon as they were passed beyond that road he sunk into a quiet phase, cutting himself off from the rest.

*****

Brining the RV to a slow, easy stop, Jermaine turned his head to see where everyone was in back. With the exception of Todd and the dogs, they were all sleeping away the tedium of the drive. He yelled back to the others "Y'all should see this." He pointed down the road to the town ahead. "Looks like this place is set up like Rivers Crossing."

Charlie, riding in the passenger seat, opened his eyes and yawned. An old school bus with sheet metal covering over the windows and lining the bottom blocked the street. With the way the metal was blocking the underside of the bus there was no way to crawl under it.

Three men, armed for war, stood in front of it motioning Jermaine to pull forward slow and easy.

"What do you think?" Jermaine asked

Pulling the map out and tracing from the last town that they had found gas at, to where he thought they were at now, Charlie replied. "Well, I guess we need to decide what it is we are looking for. Are we looking for another safe place to stay for a while or a new place to call home. If it is a place to make a home, I think we may have found an option here."

"Is this what you were expecting?" Tressa asked.

Charlie shook his head no and looked at Jermaine. "You have seen more of Bob's safe places. This what you were looking for?"

"Nah, Bob's places are usually out of the way and hidden from anyone that didn't know they were there."

Two men, with their guns trained on Jermaine and Charlie, advanced, followed by one that Jermaine thought for sure was in charge. "Exit the camper now with your hands above your head."

Jermaine raised his hand and stump up so that they could see them clearly. "We're coming out, just stay calm, mister." Turning to Charlie he whispered. "I can slam it in reverse but we can't outrun bullets."

"Everyone out like the man says, keep your hands up so that nobody gets shot." Charlie said as he raised his arms up. "Ok, we are coming out. We have four adults, two dogs, one young woman and an oversized grown man that is like a seven-year-old." Charlie glanced over his shoulder at Tressa as he slowly reached down to open the door. "Sorry for that, but I don't want them to shoot Todd if he freaks out or anything."

Before Tressa could say anything Todd pipped up. "Don't worry, Mister Charlie, I know how to play cops and robber."

Once they were all outside Virginia had the lads sit on either side of her. One man walked up and took a close look at them all, paying particular attention to their skin color. "They all look fine, but this one here may have been bitten." Another man came up and lifted Jermaine's arm up poking and prodding at the bandage. Then in a swift move ripped it off. "What happened here?"

"I was bit by a zombie that caught me off guard." Jermaine replied.

"Don't see any bite marks." The man stated.

Jermaine smiled back at the man and replied. "I cut it off so that I wouldn't turn."

"What the hell did you use to cut it off?"

"A circular saw." Jermaine replied.

"You let one of these folks cut your arm off with a circular saw?" The man asked shocked.

"No, not one of them. I cut it off." Jermaine replied stressing the *I*.

Finishing his inspection, and only pausing briefly by Virginia and the dogs, the man turned to the others. "They can pass. Someone take the gentleman on the end to see Doctor Tybor and let him see if he can clean up that mess he did to himself." Turning back around with a big smile he announced. "Welcome to the town of Nusha, you will all be safe here for as long as you chose to stay. Keep your weapons if you choose too, if you can fight we can sure use your help either as watchers on the wall or helping reclaim sections of where people coming in like yourself can take up a house and live." Turning back toward the bus blocking the road he ordered. "Captain of the guard, kindly let these good folks in and direct them to the welcome center for orientation."

"Yes sir, Major! Open the gate." Replied the Captain.

"Opening the gate." Another voice yelled as the bus came to life with a puff of black smoke. It slowly rolled backward, opening the road.

Charlie drove the RV through the gate slow so that they could all take in the town. If there were any signs of trouble, he wanted to be able to find a way back out. The armed man in front of them led the way, walking down the middle of the street, then directed Charlie to turn right on a side street. Coming up to the window he said. "If you go down about two blocks you will see the old Post office, that is now the welcome center for new arrivals. You will probably all be there for an hour or maybe two, depends on if Agnes is the one giving the talk or MaryAnn. Agnes is quick while MaryAnn will cover every possible thing like the Creator himself was passing it on to you. Just smile as she talks knowing that you only have to go through it once." He said laughing. "After that, one of them will

248

give you a map that will take you back up here to Main Street. From here you will head South until you see Belmont Street, you turn left there and you will find the houses they will give you to pick from. They may still be a mess, just to warn you ahead of time but they will be zombie free."

Charlie nodded his head that he understood when the man added. "Just so you know, we have a gal here that has a son just like the boy you have with ya. They might like to meet each other sometime."

"Thanks Sir, I am sure that Todd would love that." Charlie replied as he pressed the gas pedal making the turn.

"Looks like we have found a home." Zoe said smiling. "Wish my Albert could have seen this day."

"Doc would have been in heaven being able to work with other Doctors." Tressa added.

"He would have been in heaven just seeing this place." Charlie added. "This is what he thought Rivers Crossing would turn into."

Charlie pulled up in front of the Post office and turned the motor off.

"Looks like it is time for us to start our new lives." Jermaine said as he climbed out of the RV.

Charlie and Virginia were the last to leave the RV. Sitting there, watching children play along the street and in the yards, was just a little too much for him to take in all at once.

"You know eventually I will go find my sister. Or at the very least try to find her." Virginia stated as she moved up to the passenger seat.

"I don't even know where to begin looking." Charlie said. "By the time we could get back to that place where the highways intersected the snow will be melted."

"Maybe, but then again I think we know where she is going." Virginia replied. "If I know Lori, she will go home for a while. Especially now that she doesn't think anything can happen to her. Not like she can get infected again."

"Let's just lay up here for some time and let both you and Jermaine heal. We can use this place as a home base when we go out and look for Lori. Might be nice knowing that we have a place to come back to." Charlie said. "If we do that that, I think we have a better chance of surviving out there than you do by yourself with the dogs."

"As long as we don't forget and that is the plan." Virginia replied.

The End

Made in the USA
Lexington, KY
27 February 2018